Dreams Do Come True

The Dream Trilogy, Volume 2

Larynn Ford

Published by Larynn Ford, 2024.

DREAMS DO COME TRUE

First edition. October 8, 2024.

Copyright © 2024 Larynn Ford.

ISBN: 979-8227244420

Written by Larynn Ford.

Table of Contents

Thanks to my daughters, Stacie and Stephanie for all your help with ideas and travel arrangements. You make my life easier.

1

The Bradys chatted, sipping their morning coffee at the kitchen table. When we *breezed* into the living room, neither blinked an eye at our unusual entrance. But then again, it wasn't so unusual to them. Layne's human parents had been aware of his dual life for much longer than I.

Mrs. Brady met us in the kitchen door. "Son, it's so good to see you. And Lynzi, honey, we're so happy you decided to come along." She was busy with her own brand of multi-tasking. After hugging the two of us, she hurried back to retrieve coffee mugs for us and to tend to some other cooking she had going on the stove.

"Y'all come on in and have a seat, son. Lynzi gal, it *is* good to see you again. Mama just made a batch of fried apple pies here. Y'all help yourselves now." Mr. Brady gestured to the platter piled high with the homemade turnovers.

"Lake told me about the trouble y'all are having. What else can you tell us, Daddy?" Layne asked between bites. Concern, as well as the aroma of warm apples and cinnamon, hung heavy in the air.

"We've lost more than two dozen cows in the last week alone, son. That newest bunch of yearlings we moved over to your place is gone, too. Lake had cut out all his young bulls to take to auction next week, now they're all dead. Looks like wild animal kills to me. Massive-sized animals. The cows' throats were ripped out with one bite." Mr. Brady studied the coffee in his mug and shook his head.

"I'm sure you've already run this by Tom. What was his take on it?" Layne's brow knit closer together. His expression echoed his daddy's pain now that we had heard how serious the matter had become.

"He helped us examine and dispose of the carcasses. Some of the kills were consumed as food, but most of them seemed to be slaughtered for no reason. Just killed and left to rot where they lay. He did his own brand of investigating and agreed cats were to blame but I'm sure his people hold fast to the laws Tom set down when they moved into the area. They're our neighbors and we all look out for one another. They promised years ago to hold their hunting to the national forest area and I'm positive Tom wouldn't stand for any other behavior. It appears to be another group of cats that have moved into the area. We just can't figure out who they are or where they came from."

Mrs. Brady studied me for a minute and placed one hand on the arms of each of the men at her sides. "Layne, have you told Lynzi about any of this?"

"Well, Mama, she heard stories about the cats living in the area from her granddaddy when she was a little girl. He was the only one who ever got a good look at them. He spotted 'em several times on the edge of the fields he was plowing but since no one else ever saw much more than a blur, they weren't sure what that movement was. I confirmed her granddaddy's stories and filled in the other facts about Tom and his family." Layne reached for my hand and winked. "It wasn't a huge surprise after I revealed *my* life to her. And believe me, I learned real fast to be open and upfront about everything. She's a bit of a wildcat herself if she thinks I'm keeping secrets . . . or if someone threatens her family. I call her my little Lynx." Layne smiled and leaned down, planting a kiss on the top of my head.

He was, of course, referring to my *reaction* at having been kept out of the loop a couple of weeks ago on plans of action where the hunt for Allvis, his power-hungry cousin, was concerned.

Hell bent on destroying the life Layne and his family had built in their world and claiming the land and everything on it for his own, Allvis' reign of terror began when Layne was an infant. Layne's parents had been forced to hide him away for his well-being. He was placed with a loving couple, Will and Sara Brady. They kept him safe and raised him in the human world to be a strong, honest man.

Layne and his birth family are Fae. A magical group of people categorized as fairies by some, but not all are the Tinkerbelle variety from the children's books. They are various sizes that range from the tiny, winged creatures to full-sized beings that pass for human when need be. They all possess magical abilities and good hearts that connect them in a powerful way.

Layne and I were separated for twenty years when he was called back to his homeland to help fight Allvis' evil. Since we reunited last month, Allvis had kidnapped me on two separate occasions and set fire to the barn in the Fae world that killed several precious animals as well as a dear friend. I hated him for all of this. The very thought set my stomach to roll.

A confrontation in the form of a sword fight in my living room between Layne and Allvis had ended with Allvis' death, or so we thought. We had stepped from the room where his body lay for a moment and when we returned, he was gone. We weren't aware of anyone else on the property, but a dead body just doesn't get up and leave unassisted. We still have no clue where he is or if he's truly dead. Now, we were always looking over our shoulders for his next attack and I was afraid he could have a hand in this mess. I prayed Layne would give me some sign, any sign, that I was wrong, and we wouldn't have to deal with Allvis again but from what I was hearing, if it weren't Allvis, it could be someone equally as callous.

Being well informed was the only way to understand a situation and make good decisions and with me being brand new to this, *out of this world* life, I needed all the information and understanding I could get.

Then, there was the incident when we were on the trip to hunt down Allvis and his goons back in the Fae world. He appeared, out of the blue, making sure he stayed a safe distance from the guard team's strike zone, to taunt and tease Layne and his family. As a last jab, he had the gall to address me by name *and* threaten our future family, the baby Layne had always dreamed of having.

Layne had armed me with a handgun for protection. I knew I was out of range but nonetheless quickly emptied the gun, rapid fire, in Allvis' general direction to make my point. *Don't mess with my family.* I may be a weak, frail human female but I was a female raised in the South and we don't take kindly to anyone intending to harm our families. Allvis pulled a Fae disappearing act on us before any of my rounds could possibly make contact, bellowing a hideous, mocking laugh as he faded from our sight.

"Pet told me all about that on her last visit and I don't blame you one bit, honey. Us womenfolk have to know what's going on so we can help protect our families. And there's *nothing* wrong with being armed." She pointed to the shotgun standing in the corner by the back door. They were often kept handy in the country in case of an intruder or other emergency.

Mr. Brady's expression softened. A twinkle danced in his eyes as he gazed at his wife and covered her hand with his. I got the feeling they, also, had had a discussion or two about sharing information and how much is the right amount.

"Tom's a good man, Lynzi. Like I said, we all look out for each other around here. Tom and his family help keep the deer and rabbit population to a healthy number when they hunt but they never go after farm animals. They have farms and raise livestock, too. It's a livelihood for all of us. So, when our herds started being slaughtered, we hoped Layne could help us find out who or what was behind all this," Mr. Brady explained.

"And I brought you along because, well, first, because I can't stand to be apart from you for more than a minute or two at a time, and second because you can ask questions for me that I can't, me being dead around here and all." Layne tweaked my nose and poured more coffee for the four of us.

Layne and I were separated, worlds apart, for many years due to his responsibilities in the Fae world. Since the duties that called him home were dangerous, the human world, myself included, was led to believe he had died in an accident. When the danger bled over into my world, directed at me, Layne revealed himself as alive, we reunited, and now I am happy beyond my wildest dreams.

When Granddaddy told the tales of a huge black panther watching him plow the fields, I thought it was fascinating. I never saw the animals myself, but if my Granddaddy had seen them, that was good enough for me. Now, I learned the story was not only true but there was an unbelievable twist.

I had heard of werewolves from books and movies but of course thought them to be the fiction they were portrayed to be. I now learned that not only were they *real* but *other* werecreatures existed, too. Werepanthers, in this case. Mercy. Will wonders never cease?

"Lynzi and I are gonna walk over to Lake's place and see what he's found out. Do y'all want to walk with us?" Layne took my hand and helped me to my feet as I reached for our empty coffee mugs to take to the sink.

"No, son, I'll let you draw your own conclusions. The boss here has given me my orders for the morning. I need to get the last of the spring turnip greens in from the garden so she can get 'em washed, blanched, bagged, and in the freezer, *today*." Mr. Brady gave his wife another pat on the hand. He regarded her with the same love and adoration in his eyes as Layne's when he gazed at me.

"And this winter when you're enjoying those greens for supper, you'll be glad you listened to me, Will Brady." Mrs. Brady returned the gentle pat on his hand as she took their mugs to the sink. She turned toward Layne and added, "I'll have a little something ready to eat when you all get back. Bring Lake and the boys along and we can talk while we have lunch."

As Layne and I reached the back door, I noticed Mr. Brady had eased up behind his wife at the sink and was nuzzling her neck in much the same way his son does with me. I see the apple doesn't fall far from the tree. Will and Sara Brady may not be Fae and bound by fate, but anyone could tell they were each one the other's heart.

Layne reminded me since he was *dead* here, he would need to make himself invisible to all eyes. He assured me he would be at my side, and I could hear him and sense his presence as we walked through the pastures to investigate the scene for ourselves.

He eased his arms around my waist and tugged me close. We stood enveloped in each other's arms and swayed together to our own music. "You know, we could scan the field later. That big ol' hay loft out yonder in the barn seems to be calling our names." Layne was nibbling my earlobe as he whispered his enticements, but Lake popped in at that moment to walk over the kill sights with us.

Lake was Layne's right-hand man and head guard in the Fae world. They had known one another for many years, and each could depend on the other for anything. His company was a good idea, since I'd look like I'd lost my mind walking along alone talking to myself, but now? Seriously? Layne was coming up with one of his extraordinary ideas. We needed to do a bit of investigating then we could find a nice quiet, Lake-free zone to pick up where we left off.

"Y'all ready to go?"

By the sly grin on his face, Lake had all the confirmation he needed that he had interrupted something, again, and darned if he didn't seem to enjoy it a bit too much. Oh well, as I've told him often, pay back is a bear.

Layne shook his head and headed for the back door mumbling something about, "One of these days."

The Bradys owned just over a hundred acres on Brady Hill Road in Macon County and Lake had bought a piece of farmland across the road from them as a base of operations here in the human world. He could move animals from the Fae ranch to the location here and then to clients who had purchased them or buy animals and move them from here back to the ranch on the other side without drawing any unwanted attention.

The barn at Lake's place was as massive as the one on the ranch in our Fae world. Aunt Pet, Layne's aunt and an elder of the Fae world, an ancient, and experienced healer and spiritual person, had created a portal inside the barn. A vast magical passageway between the two worlds that allowed a truck to be *driven* from one world into another, without being seen by anyone and causing suspicion.

Layne's cousin, Cloi, and the legal team in the family's Texas oil business had arranged everything from bank accounts, deeds, and titles to social security numbers, and birth certificates to make it possible for Lake and the team to blend into human society. Like the arrangements made for my *inheritance* from Layne at the late reading of his will. His plan to make it possible for me to be able to retire early from my job and never have to worry about money again was put into place and I had done so earlier in the week. The section of land next to the Brady's was part of my inheritance so, now, the family owned all the land on Brady Hill Road.

As a landowner, I could come and go anywhere around here without any questions. To the world, my world, I was part of the Brady family because of Layne's last wishes. The Bradys had become like additional parents to me. Although the will wasn't *discovered* and read for twenty-some years after his *death*, all Layne's wishes had been honored.

My neighbor, Lake, and I had much in common with our love of animals. Now, being seen together or working together was as normal as neighbor helping neighbor. It was a sweet little set up. Very believable.

We stepped off the back porch and headed toward the scene of one of the kills. Lake stooped and surveyed the ground but shook his head indicating he couldn't read any more information than Tom Monroe or Mr. Brady had in the hours after the animals were found dead. Tom's sense of smell was almost as acute in human form as it was when he was in animal form.

"I can't sense anything, Layne, how 'bout you?" Frustration clung to every word. He sounded exasperated and worried, knowing the remaining herds on his place were in as much danger as the Brady's or any other family in the area.

"Nothing." Layne's voice was strong although only Lake and I could hear him. Aunt Pet had woven a magical shield in a small area around us to prevent anyone outside our circle from hearing him speak.

We moved on across the pasture to the next kill sight. They both surveyed the ground, still, nothing. One problem was the remains had either been burned or buried depending on the number of cows in a single kill so the scent of the decomposing animals wouldn't draw coyotes or other predators searching for an easy meal. Either way, the ground had been disturbed enough to cover most of the clues leading to the identity of the killers.

Lake crouched close to the ground again. He scratched in the dirt and pick up a few pebbles. Rolling them around in his hand, he glanced up into thin air, but I realized he was communicating with Layne.

"What have you found?" It had to be of some consequence if they were speaking with each other telepathically.

Lake spoke aloud, "I'm sorry, Lynzi. I don't mean to leave you out. Our kind of communication comes natural and I forget sometimes."

"No need for apologies." I was used to being the last to hear a conversation now and patiently waited my turn. He rolled the pebbles around in his hand and studied them for a few minutes. I could all but see the wheels turn in his head as he mulled over their meaning.

"These are not ordinary rocks. I don't know *what* they are just that they're different. I'm fairly sure they're some kind of magic."

2

"I can't quite put my finger on it, either. I think Aunt Pet should come out here and see what she thinks," Layne agreed.

If it was magic, Aunt Pet would know for sure. What kind *and* where it came from. As we continued farther across the pasture, movement in the tree line at the edge of the field caught my attention. Although I was certain I was safe from any possible harm, the sight of a massive black cat stopped me in my tracks.

I sucked in a sharp breath and gasped as I did my best to absorb the sight of the mammoth cat watching our group from the distance. I didn't want to make any sudden moves to startle him for fear he would attack. My hands shook, my heart pounded, making it hard to breathe. I swallowed hard. "Layne, Lake. The trees to the left." The super-sized cat sat inside the tree line and studied us before he stood and slipped behind the trees out of sight.

"I saw him, darlin'. I think it was Tom. But don't you worry now, you're safe." Layne circled the nape of my neck with his hand, sliding his thumb back and forth in a soothing fashion.

I reminded myself I was in the safest hands possible with a Fae warrior on either side of me, but I remained on high alert.

My desire to circle Layne's waist with my arm for my own comfort was powerful but I realized how strange that would appear to anyone watching so, I shoved my hands in my pockets to maintain a more normal air.

I couldn't believe my eyes. Was this what Granddaddy Lancaster had seen all those years ago? "Layne, he was huge."

Layne eased his arm around my waist and tucked me close to his side, assuring me I was indeed safe with him nearby.

At that moment, a man stepped from behind a tree and started toward us. Tall with broad shoulders, dark, curly, shoulder-length hair, and dark eyes, he was dressed in jeans and a white pull-over shirt that stretched across his chest as if it had been applied with a paintbrush. His smile was broad with sparkling white teeth that gleamed against his bronzed skin. He slung his hand over his head in greeting. Lake waved back and signaled our welcome. As he approached, he greeted Lake and then *Layne* as if he saw him standing with us. Layne's hand tightened on my back tugging me closer to his side.

"Lake, Layne, it's good to see you again. And you must be Lynzi. The Bradys have told me all about you. I'm Tom Monroe."

I nodded my acknowledgement. Still in mild shock, realizing I had just witnessed the same sight my granddaddy must have seen on the edge of his cornfield.

Since Tom seemed to *see* Layne, he understood I would worry the magic shield had stopped working and he would be at risk. "He has a keen sense of smell even in human form, darlin'. We're still safe and protected," Layne whispered in my ear.

His voice was reassuring but still I worried.

"Have you found anything new, Tom?" Lake took the lead in the conversation from our side. He was in serious mode now. Lake was the biggest jokester I had ever known but with the senseless slaughter of cattle in the area, I was certain he intended to get to the bottom of this mystery. He had worked hard to establish himself here on this side as a dedicated businessman and seemed determined to recover and move on from this setback.

"I have an idea but it's hard for me to believe. I've picked up a faint but familiar scent. Layne, do you remember Del Weaver?" Tom paused, allowing Layne a moment, but the instant the name was mentioned, he straightened and became rigid at my side.

I was certain he recognized the name and that his memory of this person disturbed him.

"I remember that devil, how mean he was to his family. He should have been put down years ago like the rabid animal he was for raisin' his hand to Ellen and those boys." Layne bit out the words.

It must have been a serious situation by the reaction he had to the mere mention of the name, Del Weaver.

"You don't know how many times I tried, Layne. Ellen always begged me give him another chance. Every time he left a mark on her or one of the children, I went after him. Every time she would beg me to stop." Tom paused and shook his head. "She was obsessed with him, made all sorts of excuses for his nasty ways. She promised to find a way to help him stop, even talked that crazy old mother of hers into making potions for her to try on him. They tried to mellow him out some. Make him a better person. Some of her fixes worked for a while but he always found a way out of them, always went after her, and the boys again. Finally, he got fed up with her and her trying to fix him and left the area."

He raised both hands as if to say, no Del, no problem. "I figured that was best for all concerned but then, not even a week later, she packed up the boys and took off after him. We never heard from any of them again. Now this, this has a hint of his scent." His words trailed off and he gazed over the pasture.

Mr. Brady had explained one of Tom's panther abilities included being able to retain a memory of the scent of everyone he had *ever* met so it would be easy to identify the trespassers if Tom had ever met them.

"Potions? So, when Lake mentioned magic?" What in the world were we dealing with now? My mind set of in all directions, wondering how severe this situation would get. My heart sank in my chest thinking of the new danger we might be facing now.

Lake and Tom exchanged a look.

"Ellen and her mother's family were witches, Lynzi." Tom took his time getting the words out.

I tugged my bottom lip between my teeth. Witches? The situation was already serious enough and with the slightest hint that children had been abused I formed an immediate dislike for this Del person. Now, witches? I'd seen make-believe witches on television but were the ones Tom mentioned similar in reality?

I understood a wife wanting to help her husband, but I'd learned my lessons well from Aunt Pet. A person was only as good as his heart, and it sounded like this Del was void of a good heart. I was curious as all get out to find out what happened to all of them. "You think he came back after all this time and had something to do with this slaughter? But, why? Some kind of grudge? Against the Bradys? And he didn't even know Lake or me at back then."

"I don't even want to think he has come back but this old nose doesn't make mistakes. It's Del all right. I just can't imagine what he could possibly be up to." Tom shook his head and studied the ground.

"Tom, I'm not going to begin to tell you how to handle your people. Lord knows, I haven't cleaned house over on my side as well as I'd like, but I can't stand by and allow this to continue here." Tom listened carefully, focused on the area to my left and above my head, and nodded as Layne continued. "My folks make their living here. Now, you know they don't need to work, I would be more than happy to take care of them, but they enjoy this life. It's what they know and what they're comfortable with. Lake has holdings here, too, just like Lynzi and me. If we catch him in the act on our places, he will be dealt with." Layne spoke with a calm and even flow to his words. There was no threat or blame, just a man stating facts about protecting his own.

None of this was any of Tom's doings but I read his expression. He took responsibility for everything that had happened being the leader of this panther clan.

"I understand, Layne. But I'm going to ask you as a long-time friend and neighbor to turn him over to me for panther justice. He needs to be reminded he can never go against our laws and make his own rules. We live by our own code of ethics in addition to the law of the land. I tried to abide by his mate's request and let Ellen handle her situation her way, but now he is going to pay for *everything* he's ever done . . . to her, to those boys, *and* for all this." Tom waved his hand in the direction of the charred earth, the site of the disposal of some of the dead animals.

"You have my word, Tom. I'll do my best to get him to you alive if I catch him on Brady land. Lake?" Layne waited for Lake's take on Tom's request. It was his call as to how he would handle Del if he caught him trespassing on his property.

Lake nodded. "If it's possible, you'll get him alive, Tom." He reached out to shake hands with Tom and seal their gentleman's agreement.

"Mama said she'd have lunch ready when we got done looking around out here. Tom, would you come to the house and have something to eat with us? She and Daddy need to know what you've found out and what to be on the lookout for. They'll both remember Del as well as I do." Layne kept me close to his side. Since we now had a lead, that a disturbed panther person was at the root of all this I was glad to be protected by Layne's strong arm. I kept an eye out for any movement around us in case we were about to be attacked. I had learned to expect the unexpected and always be aware of my surroundings.

"You know I never pass up your mama's good cooking, Layne." Tom joined us as we took the path back toward the house.

"Lake, call the boys. You know Mama, her *little something to eat* means she's cooked for an army." Layne rubbed gentle circles up and down my back for reassurance.

I was worried. What were we going to have to do to resolve *this* mess? How much danger was everyone in? How crazy was this Del and how far would he go to get whatever it was he was after? So many questions and thoughts ran through my mind.

Layne's reaction to my tense body told me he was aware of the questions I had, and I was certain I would have my answers soon.

3

The picnic table in the sunroom adjacent to the kitchen had been set for eleven. As I filled the glasses with ice cubes for Mrs. Brady's famous sweet tea, I counted the lunch guests, the Bradys, two guard teams, Lake, Tom, Layne, and myself. Ten. The squeak of the screen door on the back porch drew my attention as Aunt Pet glided toward the table. Ah. Eleven.

"Aunt Pet, what a surprise! I didn't know you were coming today." I greeted her with a hug.

"Hello, my little one. Yes, yes, I have been here for a short time. I have surveyed the area of the cattle kills and found some quite interesting items." As an elder of the Fae world, magic, was her life. She had studied long and hard to perfect her skills with herbal remedies aided by Fae magic. If, in fact, Lake's guess was correct, and magic was used in the pasture near the kills, Aunt Pet would be able to confirm. Excitement resounded in every word about her findings.

"Oh, that *is* good news. I'm about to call the menfolk in before all this good food gets cold. You can tell us what you found when they all get seated." I paused before going into the living room to gather the lunch crowd to the table, nervously worrying my hands together. A sick feeling knotted in the pit of my stomach, and I hesitated, but had to ask, "Aunt Pet, Tom mentioned a witch or two having lived here about some time ago. What kind of magic do you think they practiced? Are they dangerous?"

"Oh, little one, you should not worry so. I do not sense dark magic at work on this land. These are merely illusions. Illusions to cover the comings and goings of the killers." Aunt Pet never worried. She always had a trick or two up her sleeve and it was evident this situation was no exception.

Mrs. Brady had out done herself in the kitchen again. A serving bowl heaped with fresh turnip greens seasoned with strips of bacon and chopped onion sat steaming on the table. A platter piled high with golden ears of corn drenched with butter. Matching platters holding corn muffins, biscuits, and sliced beef roast rested beside another bowl filled with chunky potato salad. The sweet scent of banana pudding fresh out of the oven danced in the air.

We all gathered around the table and bowed our heads as Mr. Brady asked blessings on the food and the situation we were facing. Eight ravenous men dug in and passed the platters around the table. Not much conversation circulated while food was present on the table but as the banana pudding was being dished up, Mr. Brady asked if we had found anything new on our trip outside earlier.

Tom cleared his throat to begin to deliver the disturbing discovery. Everyone listened with pronounced interest as he recounted his findings and filled in the blanks for those who had not heard the story earlier of the abusive panther husband and father who terrorized his family for years before disappearing, never to be heard from again, or so it seemed. We all sat in silence for a bit, some absorbing the new information, some already formulating a plan to deal with the threat.

Aunt Pet nodded her agreement as Tom spoke of the spells and potions made by Ellen and her mother to curb Del's drinking and bad temper and to change his abusive behavior.

Ellen's mother was an out-and-out, card-carrying witch and her father was a full-blooded werepanther, so she possessed the abilities of both parents.

"I found evidence of magic intended to mask scents. If the killers were panthers, they knew Tom would recognize the scents and be able to identify them on the spot. I sensed three animals. All male," Aunt Pet added.

Neither of them indicated the witch had been back on the property. Tom was not sure at this point of the identity of the other two males.

"That would explain why the scents were so faint. A spell was used to hide Del's involvement. I never thought Ellen would go along with something like this." Tom sounded more frustrated by the minute.

"We could put some of the cows in the barns and the others in the pens close by. If we stake ourselves out around the barns tonight and wait, maybe they'll show up again. They won't be expecting the likes of us waiting for them." Lake indicated himself and the other Fae guards seated around the table. They were experienced warriors and skilled in battles far greater than facing a few renegade cats. He sounded determined to put an end to this as soon as possible.

"Sounds like a plan. Lynzi and I will move our stock before we come in for supper. After we eat, we can station ourselves around the barns. Tom, will your folks be ready by then?" Layne spelled out his ideas to add to Lake's plan.

Tom had more than fifty panthers under his leadership and over half that number were full grown or young adults who could handle themselves in a sticky situation. I couldn't imagine meeting a mature werepanther face-to-face and I sure wouldn't want to be on their bad side at the time.

"We'll be ready. I'm going to go call a meeting and fill everyone in on what we've found. Del *is not* welcomed back here. He made enemies of all my people long before he left, and we all want this senseless slaughter to end." Tom excused himself from the table after expressing his thanks and praising Mrs. Brady again for the fine meal she had fixed to go deliver the news of Del's return and make plans to rally his troops into action.

To keep their presence a secret, Lake and the guard teams offered their thanks and disappeared directly from the table so no one outside the room would know their location. Layne and his daddy went to the living room to talk and left the three women to clean up the kitchen. Hmm, some things never change no matter what world you're in.

"Well, we best get at it," I said as I stood and began collect the plates from the table.

"Sit, little one. Sit." Aunt Pet waved her hands in a nonchalant motion and the dishes . . . *took themselves* to the kitchen. They rose and floated from the table to the countertop. In the short time it took to travel that distance, they were cleaned, stacked, and ready to be put away. I eased back down into my chair, amazed at what I had witnessed. Olive helped around the house in the Fae world and had always cleared the table at the ranch in a more traditional manner, or so I thought.

Mrs. Brady chuckled as she reached over and gave me a little hug. "Honey, the first time she did that here it scared the living daylights out of me. I had seen Layne move things as a child and it was always somewhat unnerving, but I got used to it." She and Aunt Pet shared a glance and giggled.

I had at least managed to close my mouth by this time. "I *know* what you mean. I should be used to tasks being completed by non-manual methods by now, but somehow it always takes me by surprise."

Aunt Pet held up both hands in an, *oh, it's no big deal* manner. We all laughed.

"And what's so funny in here?" Layne stood behind my chair and began a slow, gentle massage of my neck and shoulders. His fingers working magic of their own.

"Aunt Pet was lending a helping hand with the dishes is all," I answered, trying my best not to slip into a message trance and moan out loud.

"Well, Lynzi and I are going to go to our place for a while and check on things there. We should be back in a few hours. Mama, what can we do to help with supper?" Feeding this bunch was a grand production and neither of us wanted to tire his mama out by saddling her with all the cooking chores.

"Pet and I have everything under control for supper, son. Your daddy is going to grill some chickens outside and we'll take care of the rest."

"I can bake a peach cobbler at home and bring it when we come back. I think we have everything I need to make some homemade vanilla ice cream, too." I was more than happy to contribute something to the evening meal.

From her pleased expression, Mrs. Brady was just glad to have Layne home again. "Well, thank you, Lynzi honey, peach cobbler and ice cream sound real good."

Because I was known in these parts now as a landowner and part-time resident, it wasn't a strange sight for me to be seen anywhere in the area. How I arrived would seem strange if I didn't do it in the traditional method of driving some sort of vehicle, so I kept a truck hidden in the barn at Lake's to make my arrival appear more *normal*. We would transport into his barn and drive out to the road to go where we needed. Lake had parked it here earlier, so I climbed in and made my way down the road to our house where Layne was waiting for me inside.

"I made a sweep of the barn before I came in and everything's normal." Layne was already reaching for me as I closed the front door.

A constant, unbelievably strong urge to be in close contact with each other made it difficult to be apart for *any* length of time. This need grew stronger with each day we were together. He had explained it was the Fae bond. Heart to heart. We needed to be near to absorb the other's warmth, breathe the same air, and it was fine with me. We had years to make up for and I didn't want to miss a single moment of our time together.

We moved to the couch and settled down for some quiet time. My mind wandered to the plan for tonight and I worried about everyone's safety. A knot had formed in the pit of my stomach when I began hearing all these new and strange events. Now, it swelled, slowly increasing in size. "Layne, what do you think will happen if Del and the other cats come back tonight?"

"We'll try to hold 'em off until Tom can get there if it's possible. But, darlin', you know what happens to animals when they go bad."

I did. An animal that started killing farm stock had to be put down. Wild animals as a rule kept to themselves only killing to survive and then moving on. Pets sometimes turn bad or for some reason are born with a kill habit. In either case, a wild animal that made a nuisance of himself or a bad-mannered pet that begins to kill has to be moved out of the area or be put down. It was sad to be sure, but still, a simple fact of country life.

Tom had explained, it was a much different story in the case of animals that spent a good deal of their time as humans and understood right from wrong. These animals have their own code to live by as well, and if they choose to defy the code, they must pay the price. They would face a tribunal of their own people who would hear both sides, decide if a wrong had been done, and abide by the ruling. If we were lucky enough to catch Del, I had been assured he would pay for everything he had done to his wife and children and to the good name of the panther clan that had made their home here for decades.

"I know all this has you uneasy, darlin', but you'll be safe."

Layne could read me like a book. I was troubled but I didn't worry about my safety since I would be inside the house with his parents and Aunt Pet. My concern was for him and the boys. He was my heart, and they were like brothers to me.

They had experience fighting other Fae beings, I had seen as much in the confrontations with Allvis' gang a few weeks ago. Layne's cousin had caused much trouble in the Fae world. He had to be stopped from his power-hungry ways and pay for the crimes he had committed. Yet, I wondered how much experience they had going up against panthers as big as some of the yearlings that had been slaughtered.

"You know I'm not worried about me." I snuggled closer under his arm and slid my arms around his waist. I wanted to protect *him* from any harm. "It's just . . . first I learned of the Fae and other beings from your world, now werecreatures, *and* witches here in the human world, what else is out there, Layne? What else do we have to worry about?" I realized that not only did we have to continue to watch over our shoulders for Allvis, but now these other beings, too.

Werepanthers *and* witches? What had I allowed myself to get into?

4

I had experienced one of the Fae special *abilities* several times with Layne's Fae mama. When I had been upset, her touch or even the sound of her voice had a special calming effect on me. Layne shared that ability with her. His protective nature was in play now as he was trying to be honest with me about all the things that go bump in the night, but at the same time, ease my fears. He adjusted our bodies to a more comfortable, reclining position.

"Well, darlin', there *are* others out there. All those stories and tall tales you've heard all your life and the documentaries on television about strange or unexplained happenings around the world have *some* truth to them. There are mysterious animals, witches, mystical, or magical folk in one way or another. People tend to stretch the truth, but all those stories *do* have a factual basis." He adjusted his hold on me and continued in the same even, calming tone. "What you have to realize, sweetheart, is that just as it is with humans or animals, there's good and bad everywhere. Tom's people are good folks who happen to be panthers some of the time. Del is one of those born with a mean streak. He is plain bad with not an ounce of good in him."

He paused for me to absorb the news of the existence of the other beings. "Why don't you try to get a nap now? Everything will be clearer after you rest." Layne tugged me closer into a reassuring hug and kissed the top of my head, the same head that was trying to process all the new information about the actual existence of *others* in my world.

With a light touch, he placed his thumb in the center of my forehead signaling one of his sweet dreams was in my near future. I relaxed, closed my eyes, and tried to push the unknown from my mind by counting my true blessings. I had two beautiful daughters, all grown up and making a life of their own. The man of my dreams, one I adored, and who was truly devoted to me. Not just one but two sets of in-laws I loved as much as my own parents, ones who in turn loved and accepted me as their only daughter. I had many wonderful friends in both worlds. All this was new and strange to me, but it was *my* life nonetheless, and I wouldn't trade it for anything.

A SOFT BREEZE DRIFTED across the river, cooling the air as the warm summer day ended. Stars sparkled like diamonds in the crystal-clear night sky. The new moon hung low on the horizon. Its mellow orange reflection shimmered across the water's surface. I took a deep breath. The cool night air filled my lungs and relaxed my tense body. Crickets chirped. Frogs sang their evening song. Fireflies danced in every direction. The waves rocked the couch in a soothing rhythm. I was cradled in Layne's strong arms.

"Layne, we're dreaming." I had learned to expect the dreams now. It was another Fae *ability* Layne, and his people possessed—controlling, or influencing dreams. The dreams Layne shared with me were always pleasant, peaceful, and relaxing. Each one was more wonderful and exciting than the last.

Some couples talk about the future they want together, Layne displays ours in brilliant color, with all the other senses likewise as vivid. I had no doubt this dream would be as dazzling and enlightening as every other one had been.

"Mmm-hmm. How do you like the river?" He waved his hand to indicate the beautiful moonlit scene before us. We were still on the couch from our living room but as I glanced around, I found the couch was on a raft . . . a raft floating in the middle of the river. It was decorated with floral garland on all sides. The coffee table was set with a tray holding two glasses of Aunt Pet's homemade rosebud wine. We sipped the light, sweet pink wine as the fireflies danced closer to the raft.

"See, darlin', while there's bad in every life, there's good, too. And you and I have so much more good than bad. Take a look." He pointed toward the flutters of light all around us.

I studied the fireflies. Their glittery wings sparkled in the moonlight. They smiled and sang a happy song. But they weren't fireflies. They were my dainty Fae friends. The ones that go with me and watch over me when Layne's not around, ready to call him to my side in an instant if need be. They settled on the garland surrounding the raft and illuminated it as if miniature electric lights had been flicked on.

As we drifted along, I heard voices from the banks on both sides of the river. On our left, the Bradys sat in rocking chairs on their front porch. They waved and smiled as they enjoyed glasses of sweet, iced tea. Across the river stood the barn from the ranch. Tad waited in front and waved to us as the animals frolicked around his feet.

Farther down the river, Twig took a break from his work in my rose garden to tip his cap to us. Aunt Pet blew a kiss in our direction as she lounged in an oversized porch swing hung in the shade from the limb of a tall oak tree. My beautiful black mare, Star, galloped along the bank followed by her spunky baby boy. The guard teams swung from a rope tied high to a tree limb and landed cannonball style in the water near our raft, doing their best to drench the two of us. Layne's Fae mama and daddy, Lark and Laynaro smiled as they strolled along together down a shaded lane. Everyone was so happy and content.

Happy tears filled my eyes. My heart was so full of love. Every good memory I had about my life with Layne was displayed right before me. The good times do outweigh the bad. It was a wonderful life, and I couldn't allow the bad parts get the best of me. I was a fighter, and I would do whatever it took to make my life with Layne the best possible.

Layne hugged me and sighed. "A good life takes work, and we make the best team, you and me."

We sipped our wine and continued our dream trip down the river in the cool night air chatting about our wonderful life and our bright future together.

NOT MANY THINGS ARE better than a snuggle-nap with the love of your life, unless you count waking up from said nap to the aroma of warm peach cobbler. I had worried myself to sleep on the couch but experienced a dream that put our life into perspective. Good and bad. I'd never complain about sleeping in the arms of the man I adored. But, had the peach cobbler baked magically?

"Mmm, that smells so good. How'd you do that? Your own special, *magical* recipe?" I raised both arms high over my head and stretched to wake up. Layne stared at me with that *cute as a bug's ear* expression of his. "What? Oh no, my hair must be a mess." I started to finger comb and smooth the tangles from my hair.

"You could never be a mess, my darlin' Lynzi. And I'd like to take full credit for the cobbler but, to be honest, you were sleeping so sweet I couldn't bring myself to wake you up, so I asked Olive if she could come and lend a hand. She found your ice cream churn and put some on, too. It should be hardened by now." Layne always thought of everything. "Lake should be here in a few minutes to help with the cows."

"Y'all are so sweet. Thank you for the nap, and the dream and the dessert assistance. I do have *so* many things to be thankful for." I continued my thanks with a big hug that led the way for Layne to ease me back down on the couch for some extended snuggle time, but as soon as I heard Lake's truck roaring down the driveway, I decided it was time to head to the kitchen and offer my help.

"Okay, I'm gonna go thank Olive and I'll meet you two out back." I opened the front door for Lake and scooted off to the kitchen.

Olive had wrapped containers of homemade vanilla ice cream in newspaper and packed them in an ice chest to keep cold. The cobbler was wrapped in foil and ready to go to the Brady's as well.

"Olive, thank you so much. Layne shouldn't have bothered you. One day, real soon, I want the two of us to go for a girl's day out. Shopping, lunch, maybe a movie? We'll have a great time. What do you say?"

"Sounds like fun, Lynzi, but I love to cook, and I don't mind a bit helping out." She was still shy but enjoyed some girl time every now and then.

The Fae could read a person's heart, so I was certain she understood my words were straight from my heart.

I took her up on her offer to transport the dessert items to the Brady house and headed outside to catch up with Layne and Lake and help set up our part of the plan for tonight.

When the cows were secured for the evening, Lake and I drove back to the Brady's for supper. Olive had worked her magic in the Brady kitchen and helped get everything ready for the evening meal.

The boys were at the table and ready to eat as soon as everyone else could be seated. Two over-sized trays piled high with grilled chicken halves glazed with honey barbeque sauce, orange, and lemon slices sat on the table. Baked potatoes with all the trimmings, baked beans, and homemade biscuits sat steaming nearby.

When supper was done and the dishes had been cleared, we went over the patrol plan for the night one last time. Lake and a guard would station themselves in the loft of the barn at his place. Woods and Forrest would be at our place in an inconspicuous location and Layne and the last guard would be here at the Brady's. Tom's clan would be hidden high in the trees along the entire perimeter of the three properties.

The three humans would wait inside the house for safety's sake. No arguments from me. I shuddered when I imagined meeting a panther face to face in the dark. Let alone a giant werepanther with a grudge. Lake and the guard teams faded from the kitchen to seclude themselves in the barns they would be protecting. Tom had phoned and said his clan would be heading out for their assigned spots at dusk.

Layne took my hand and curled me close into one of his body enveloping embraces. He leaned down, buried his face in the curve of my neck, and nuzzled his favorite spot beneath my ear. "Promise me you will stay in the house until I get back, Lynx. I'm not at all sure what we're gonna be up against. I have no idea how insane Del is now or who he may have helping him with his plan." He held on tight.

Although I tried my best to control it, my voice quivered. "I promise I'll be good and stay inside if *you* promise to get this done and get back in here to me as soon as you can, *and* without a single scratch on you. Layne, if Del and his friends are as big as Tom was in his cat form today, they could cause some serious damage with hardly any effort." Each time he left me, I feared something bad would happen, and he wouldn't or couldn't come home. Layne sensed the intensity of my concern, courtesy of our heart-to-heart connection. I didn't want to see anyone get hurt tonight but I did want this situation to come to an end. Soon. I was ready for some more peace and quiet. Lots more peace and quiet.

Layne gazed deep into my eyes. "Try not to worry, sweetheart. Del has got to be stopped. He'll run us all out of business if he's not. He should have been put down long ago. And you know if a cat gets too close to me, I'll slip right out of his way." He tweaked my nose and gathered me close again. "I need to get into position before the action starts.

"Action? Layne Brady! You are itching to get into a scrap with those cats, aren't you?"

5

I wiggled free of his embrace, propped my hands on my hips, and waited for him to answer. He sounded as if he would *risk* getting hurt if it meant he could be the one to teach Del a lesson or two about how *not* to treat your family. Lessons he well deserved but would fight to avoid and not care who he hurt in the process.

He drew me to his chest and shushed my fears. "Well now, darlin', I sure wouldn't mind giving ol' Del a taste of his own medicine. He sure was mean to those little boys of his. Some men just don't know a blessing when they have it right in the palms of their hands." Layne's hands happened to have slid down my back and were now *palming* my behind, but I knew he had other blessings in mind, too, and we would have those, one of these days.

"Very funny, Layne Brady." I inched in closer, pressing our bodies tighter together to make sure he realized what he was leaving to go cat hunting. He held his head back a bit and closed his eyes. Not only because of my subtle reminder, but also because someone was communicating with him mentally. After a few seconds, he opened his eyes and gazed down at me.

"What is it, Layne?" I prayed it wasn't bad news already.

"Lake told me everyone is in position, and all is quiet. They may not show at all tonight, darlin', but I need to get to my station and do my part." He kissed the tip of my nose and rested his forehead against mine. "I promise I'll be careful."

Sucking in a determined breath, I gave him one last kiss and stepped aside to allow him to fade out into the night.

I stared out the door into the early spring evening. Everything appeared normal. *Normal.* Did I even know the meaning of the word anymore?

A gentle hand cupped my elbow. "He'll be fine, honey. Now, don't you be frettin' so much. I made a fresh pot of coffee, why don't we sit at the table and talk while we have a cup? I found something the other day that had been packed away years ago and we thought you might like to see."

Mrs. Brady always seemed to understand what was bothering me. It was like she had some sixth sense of her own. Or maybe it was *her* good heart in tune with mine. We both worried about Layne's safety.

I gathered the mugs and cream and headed to the table where Mr. Brady shuffled through a cigar box of old photos.

"We thought you'd like to see Layne as a boy growing up here on the farm. Here's one we took the first time he drove the tractor. He was four." Mr. Brady's face beamed with pride as he examined the picture. Perched up on that big ol' John Deere tractor was a skinny, dark-haired farmer boy dressed in overalls, and sporting a proud grin.

We sipped our coffee as we made our way through the entire box of Brady memories. Pictures from the time Layne came to live here as an infant through his high school and army years. "There are no pictures of high school prom or dances here. He must have dated before we met. Don't I get to see what my competition was?" I was a wee bit curious.

"Oh no, honey. Layne got rid of all those pictures. I figure it was just about the time he met you." Mrs. Brady patted my hand and winked. She reached into the box and took out a tattered notepad, handed it to me, and said, "You'll see."

I opened the book and found a log Layne had kept helping track regular maintenance for his truck and the machinery used here on the farm. The dates began about the time he returned home from the army but several torn edges of paper close to the binding indicated missing pages. The next page had my name, phone number, and the directions to my parent's house. On the line underneath were the words *this one's a keeper*, ending with a trail of tiny hearts.

Yep. The man had drawn hearts next to my name. My finger played with the ragged remnants of paper where the missing pages had been as my brow knit together in thought. The corners of my mouth inched slowly upward as I realized . . . no one else mattered. Our hearts were one from the beginning. We were together now, and a fantastic, everlasting future lay ahead for us.

"I figure he left the most important things in his book . . . his truck and you." Mr. Brady chuckled as he gathered the photos and placed them back into the box with loving care. He had echoed my thoughts to the letter.

The startling screams of panthers pierced the night. I drew in a sharp breath. The three of us almost jumped out of our skins when we heard the growling, roaring big cat sounds. I bit my bottom lip and held my breath as I turned to the Bradys to see if I needed to be concerned. "What do you think? Good panther or bad?"

"It's hard to tell, gal. Tom and his clan are never that vocal. They've never wanted to call any amount of attention to themselves." Mr. Brady had eased up from the table and started for the door with Mrs. Brady and me close on his heels. "I've never been scared to go outside at night before. I was safe even when Tom's folks prowled and hunted in the area, but now . . . I don't know what that crazy Del has up his sleeve."

Searching for clues out the window didn't tell us much since it was well after dark, but the moon was bright and lit the yard well enough for us to see the path to the barn. A ruckus coming from behind it indicated a huge catfight, then, silence. "What do you think?" I worried Layne was in the middle of all the commotion. My chest tightened and my stomach cramped.

"I wish I knew, gal. I didn't hear any cows so maybe Tom prevented any more loss." Mr. Brady was plenty worried although he tried his best to hide it from us.

Something slinked around the corner of the barn, catching our attention as it made its way toward the house. "Is that a panther? Can you tell if it's Tom or some of his family?" It was strange that a cat would come toward the house. If it was one of Tom's clan, we had no way of communicating with them. He continued right on up to the door of the screened porch before he stopped. He was big. Sleek and black. And big. "He could take that door off the hinges with a single swipe of one of those paws."

"You're right, but I can't tell who it might be, gal. He's blocky and muscular so I'd say male, but I don't think it would be Tom. He wouldn't come to the house in cat form and not be able to talk to us." Mr. Brady kept a watchful eye on the cat while scanning the entire backyard in case this was part of some plan of attack on Del's part.

The curious cat peered through the door at the three of us, cocking his head side to side as if he expected an invitation to come inside. He lowered his body to the ground and rolled over on his back in a playful, docile gesture, wiggling around in the grass.

"Well, would you look at that," Mrs. Brady said, as surprised as I was to see the cat offering his belly in submission. "Will, what do you make of it? I've never seen any of Tom's people walk right up to the house in cat form before, let alone act so playful."

"We'll need to ask Tom. I've never seen anything like it either and I don't see or hear anything else. It looks like he's here on some business of his own."

The cat rolled again and sprang to his feet. He slapped at the air with his paw the way house cats do when they are playing with a tuft of yarn dangling from a string. *This* playful kitty was two hundred pounds if he was an ounce, though.

"He doesn't seem to be a crazed killer. I wonder what he'd do if we opened the door a wee bit?" I was curious, but I remembered the words *curiosity* and *cat* never came to a favorable conclusion when used together. There was sure something different about this cat. It was as if he wanted to tell us something. "If he is one of Tom's clan, why doesn't he change and tell us his news?"

"I don't think opening the door is a good idea, Lynzi gal. We can't be sure this isn't some sorta trick. Besides, that boy of mine would never forgive me if I let something happen to his best girl." Mr. Brady put his arm around my shoulder and gave me a squeeze.

"And as far as changing right here before us, you do realize that fur of theirs turns into skin and not clothes, right?" Mrs.

Brady placed two fingers over her lips and giggled a bit as she filled me in on another werepanther fact of life.

I covered my mouth with my hand. "Oh. I do see where that might be a bit embarrassing for all of us." We turned back to the playful panther to see what was next. He continued his antics as we watched, putting on a cute kitty act for us.

"What are y'all looking at?" Layne's voice came from behind us and startled the heck out of all of us. I almost jumped out of my skin. He had popped in from his post at the barn and was sitting at the table sipping coffee as if nothing was going on.

"Come take a look at this, son. Tell us what you think." Mr. Brady motioned out the door. "This cat has been out there for a few minutes just, playing."

As soon as Layne stepped toward the door, the cat turned and ran off behind the truck.

"Huh. Guess he just wanted to play with us."

"I can't rightly say what he was doing, Daddy. I could go find Tom, but all his folks are still in cat form and in their positions. I just popped in to check on y'all and get me some sugar." Layne leaned down and kissed me with a loud smacking sound. "Mmm-mmm. Sweet sugar."

I slid my arms around his neck and moved in closer, pressing against his strong chest. "It sure is cowboy. But, Layne, that was so weird. Well, not that any of this is what one would call normal, but *that* was *way* weird. We were afraid it was some kind of trick." I wanted that cat to continue his entertaining show so Layne could see for himself. Why had he disappeared when Layne moved toward the door?

"I know, darlin'." Layne tugged me close into one of his big bear hugs to assure me he believed us and was being serious. "And thank you for not going outside to investigate for yourself. That would be much too dangerous."

"Oh, yes, I know . . . and besides . . . your daddy wouldn't let me." I buried my face in his chest, let my voice trail off as I hurriedly spoke the last few words, and squeezed my eyes shut a bit, waiting for my inevitable scolding.

Layne blew out an exasperated breath as he shook his head and swayed side to side, rocking me in his arms. "What am I going to do with you, girl? Thank you for keeping her inside and safe Daddy. I told you she was a little wildcat herself, didn't I?"

"Now you understand what I've been dealing with all these years, son." Mr. Brady smiled wide as he pulled his own sweetie close. "I guess the old song was right. You found a girl like the girl that married your old Dad."

Knowing both my new mamas, if everyone truly believed that then I considered it a great compliment.

"So, are you done for the night?" I was eager for some good news from this mission.

"'Fraid not, darlin'. We had an attempt on the stock out back, so we need to keep on our toes. We'll be on watch till daybreak so you should try to get some sleep. None of us can afford to lose any more cows. It's just not right." Layne closed his eyes, leaned down to touch our foreheads together, and adjusted his embrace to envelope me further if that was possible.

"I know, and I understand, but you know I don't like to sleep without you. How long do you think all this can go on?"

"Could be days, sweetheart. Del was always an unpredictable ol' cuss. My guess is he's only changed for the worse. Tell you what. You go climb into bed, curl up in that cute little ball you like to sleep in, and I'll pop in from time to time tonight and check on you. Deal?"

"Mmm, I'll take what I can get for now, but I hope Del gets caught tonight. I want a regular day to day life with you, and my family, and friends, and the animals, and the ranch, here or there." I put on my brave, sincere face, but I had to force it a bit.

"We *can* have it all, darlin'. After breakfast, we'll go back to the ranch until tomorrow night. We'll spend nights here and the remainder of our time there. You can check on your animals and spend time at the barn. And you and I will have as much time alone together as we want." He raised his eyebrows and waited for me to agree to his plan.

I didn't want to sound like a crybaby about being without Layne near or keep the Bradys up past their bedtime so after one more long kiss and a promise he would be careful, Layne disappeared back to the barn to keep watch for the renegade panthers.

Screaming growls from the woods in the distant set my nerves on edge. I stared out the back door into the night. Was that Del warning us he was near and moving in for another kill?

6

Not wanting to interrupt the make-out session that had developed by the kitchen door, the Bradys had whispered their goodnights, and slipped off to their own bedroom.

I made my way to Layne's old room and settled myself into bed. It took a bit for me to drift off without my snuggle bunny to cuddle with, but I managed.

Several times during the night, I woke to find Layne sitting on the side of the bed watching me sleep. He had the face of an angel with eyes that told me I was cherished without a word spoken. He would brush my cheek with his fingertips and whisper, "Go back to sleep, darlin'." Each time, his thumb would come to rest on my forehead indicating he was giving me another sweet dream.

Heavenly sights, sounds, and smells from the ranch filled my dreams each time. In some, our family and friends worked and played around the house and barn, the animals romped in the barnyard and pastures. Always the most precious scenes of Layne and a little dark-haired, freckled-faced boy fishing at the pond or riding horses or swimming in the river. Layne's son. His dream. Our dream. And what a dream it was.

On his last visit before dawn, he slid under the covers and curled up against me. I wiggled my way into my comfort zone.

"Mmm, nothing in the world can compare to your soft skin when you slide up next to me like this, sweetness. I sure did miss you."

I inched even closer. "You were with me in my dreams. But I agree, I prefer you in the flesh, too." I rolled over to face my sweet Layne. As I adjusted the covers, I could see he planned to stay for a while on this visit and was, *excited,* about the idea.

"Did y'all make any progress last night? Please tell me we are bad cat free." I was anxious for this to be over and without any of the people I care about getting hurt.

"Well, darlin', Tom's gonna meet us downstairs for breakfast and explain the plan. Do you really want to hear the same story twice?" A sheepish grin accompanied his question as he eased himself over me and nuzzled that spot in the curve of my neck that always rendered me breathless and thus speechless. My body welcomed his touch, inviting more. I didn't need any magical abilities to determine he had a plan of his own and I was a major part of it all.

My face was slightly flushed when we reached the kitchen, and I saw everyone was already settled at the table waiting for us. Layne tried his best to cover for our tardiness. "Mornin'. Sorry y'all, we . . . overslept."

"Humph, y'all do that a lot." Lake frowned.

"Well, good morning to you, too, Lake. Ouch, do I hear a touch of frustration this morning?" I patted him hard on the shoulder as I passed to take my seat at the table.

Layne burst into laughter. Lake was having some difficulties with his latest girlfriend. She was nice enough to be sure, but she didn't seem to want the same things as Lake did out of life. She was a true city girl with no inclination of living life on a ranch. His dream for the future was much like Layne's. He had come to love country life and agreed it was the best place to raise a family. This, he was serious about. Oh, he was a jokester for sure which meant one thing was certain: life with Lake would never be dull.

"You will never learn, will you, Lake? I've told you before, my woman don't play." Layne continued to chuckle as he leaned over, kissed my cheek, and eased himself into the chair.

"Breakfast looks so good. Good morning, everybody." Platters of breakfast foods covered the table. More than enough guilt washed over me since I didn't get here sooner to help with the cooking, but as soon as Olive popped in from the kitchen to bring a platter piled high with hot, buttered biscuits I breathed a sigh of relief. Everything was under control.

As the food disappeared and everyone was satisfied, Tom cleared his throat and began to recount his experience from last night. "We made contact with Del last night, and we are certain now he's the one causing all the trouble. We spotted three cats coming out of the woods behind Lake's place about an hour after dark. We caught up with them behind the barn here and tied up in a scrap for a few minutes before they escaped back into the woods."

Tom reached for another biscuit and opened the jar of peach preserves. "They split off thinking they'd lose us, but we kept after them. I was behind Del, so I made sure *not* to let him slip away. I chased him better than a mile before he went up a tree and changed to human form. I thought he wanted to talk, so I changed, too. He blames me for causing Ellen to follow him. Says *I* encouraged her to try all those potions on him. He left here with one of those girls from Sawmill Road. She's a witch, too. Said he was going to come back after the boys, but Ellen showed up and started trying to *fix* him again."

Tom shook his head as he added a dollop of butter to his biscuit. "Now he intends to cause so much ruckus around here it'll call attention to my clan. He plans to kill off all the livestock on the road, put a hurtin' on us all financially, and run us all out of business."

Tom paused and drew a long sip from his cup before he continued. "I asked about Ellen. He just laughed as he changed back to panther form, jumped down from the tree, and disappeared into the woods. Now, I'm worried. I'm not sure what's happened to her."

Tom lowered his head and moved his eggs around on his plate with his fork. I sensed his remorse about the situation but, from all we had learned, Del was the only one to blame.

Everyone was silent for a moment and then Layne spoke. "Do you think his boys are with him or maybe, some others?"

"We're pretty sure it's them. My boys used to play with them when they were young and have retained their scents. We'll keep after them until we get them. I promise we won't let you folks down." He made eye contact with everyone at the table to seal his promise.

"It was hard for me to tell one cat from another out there last night. I don't know how much good we can be if we can't be sure who's who." Lake was back in serious mode now. "Tom, how would you feel about you and your folks sitting out tonight and let us stand watch?"

"What do you have in mind, Lake?" Tom sounded open to suggestions.

"If we have only three cats to watch out for, we could pick them off without being afraid we might be killing you or one of your family," Lake offered. "This could all end tonight."

We waited for Tom to respond. Lake's idea made perfect sense. All this could be over in one night if Lake and the boys were allowed to hunt Fae style. Arrows would be quick and silent, and these skilled hunters never missed their targets. Although I didn't like the idea of killing a living, breathing being, I wanted this nightmare over. It was sometimes necessary, and the necessity was made clearer to me when I'd been forced to kill two of the thugs working for Allvis a couple of weeks ago to protect members of my family. Sometimes, it *had* to be done.

"I know none of you owe me anything, but, as friends, I'd like a few more days to try and catch Del myself. He has to be held responsible for *everything* he's done, and I have to be the one to put an end to all this. I'm responsible for not ending it sooner and saving everybody a lot of grief." Tom was still determined to end this on his terms. My guess? An alpha male sorta thing. He didn't want to be seen as less of a leader in the eyes of his people if someone else had to solve this problem.

Silence hung in the room. Layne directed his attention to Lake, giving him the lead in the decision. Without a moment's hesitation, Lake responded, "We gave our word we'd give you the time you need, and we intend to hold true to our promise."

Layne placed both hands on the table. "That being said, everyone needs to get some rest before we go out again tonight. Lynzi and I are going back to the ranch to check on her animals there, but we'll be here before dark. Tom, if you think of anything else, Lake can get a message to me."

I could tell Layne was tired. Spending some time at the ranch would relax him somewhat. With the time difference between our two worlds, we would spend days at the ranch before nightfall came here.

We all went our separate ways until another watch would begin at dusk. Layne and I settled inside the barn at the ranch. He must have known I would want to check on my animals first. He had presented me with a barn full of miniature animals as an engagement present. Three spotted, potbelly piglets, a pair of miniature horses, Hoss and Belle, along with their baby that I named Trigger, and a flock of banty chickens. I was eager to spend some time with them.

Since time progressed at a much different pace in the two worlds, many days had passed here since we left for the Brady's. The piglets had grown so much in what seemed like a short time.

Mama was keeping true to her promise to take care of the petting and cuddling chores in my absence. "Hello, you two. How is the situation at the Brady's?" She was sitting in the piglet's stall, doling out the belly rubs to the three babies. All seemed to enjoy the attention. Her voice was melodic. Flowing and soothing, it complemented her given name, Lark. She had the ability to calm my nerves with her touch or just the sound of her voice and now it had the same effect on the animals. They gravitated to her at a single word.

"Things are still unresolved, I'm afraid. We have to go back and continue the hunt. How are my piggies?" I couldn't wait to get my hands on them.

"They are wonderful. This one is my best buddy. He loves to be held." She cuddled the smallest of the trio who ate up all the affection. "The baby girl snoozing in the corner with the round tummy reminds me of the Pooh Bear on one of your T-shirts and the mischievous one on the bale of hay climbs like a monkey. She has lots of energy." She giggled at the sight of the three special piglets.

"Sounds to me like they have the perfect names. Buddy, Pooh, and Monkey, and I couldn't have chosen better."

Layne's expression mellowed at the sight of his mama having such a good time with the piglets. "Darlin', I have to go check in with Daddy and the other guards. You two gonna be okay here for a bit?" He motioned for two of the guards to take up positions at the barn doors. Since Allvis had set fire to the barn a few weeks ago, the guards kept closer than normal.

"Of course we will. I want to play with Trigger before we leave again. And you must be dog-tired. I'll catch up with you before you settle down for a nap."

He circled my waist with his hands and lifted me off the barn floor to bring our lips together as he whispered, "How 'bout you catch up with me in the shower in about an hour?"

"Ooo, it's a date, cowboy." I mouthed the words. His touch left me breathless.

With my feet back to the floor, he propped me against the stall door with care until I could steady myself.

"The clocks ticking, fifty-nine minutes," I said.

"Yes, Ma'am. I'm going." He vanished.

I lowered myself to the hay with my new piglets and wondered when all the madness would end.

The day here had begun with Layne's surprise. Recalling a comment I had made on our first date more than twenty years ago about wanting a little farm of my own one day, he presented me with miniature animals to fulfill my wish.

Now, I wished the whole Del situation would go away so I could enjoy my animals, but I feared the trouble had only just begun.

7

The scene from last night replayed in the Brady kitchen. Werepanthers and Fae warriors stationed themselves outside to guard the livestock and hunt for renegade cats while the humans stayed tucked inside behind closed doors and away from any possible danger.

The conversation was always informative. I was rightly curious about what to expect as the human mother of a Fae child since Layne and I were talking more about our future family. The wedding was coming up in about a week and a half and we could think of no good reason for waiting to welcome a baby into the world.

Only a few weeks old when Layne came to live with the Brady family, they weren't sure when to expect his *abilities* to blossom. Layne had not kept them waiting long. Even at the infant stage of development, he was well able to transport from where he should be to where he wanted to be.

"Lynzi, honey, I don't want to scare you and make you decide against having children, 'cause Lord know we would love to have a yard full of grandbabies running around here, but I spent many hours looking from room to room for that little stinker when he decided he didn't want to be alone in his crib." Mrs. Brady chuckled. Her gaze drifting into the space above her head.

"Life must have been interesting," I said.

"Pet brought a full staff of sitters from the other side to assist in keeping Layne safe and occupied. At first, until I got used to them being here, I had to be careful not to swat the tiny critters that fluttered all over the house keeping watch over Layne."

In his efforts to ease any concerns on my part, Layne had assured me when our son *or* daughter was born, we would have more than enough help to keep him *or* her safe.

"I just hope I'm as good at handling a disappearing baby as you were." We laughed and I moved to the counter to refill the coffee mugs for our group when a strange scratching sound coming from the back porch drew my attention. The Bradys and I regarded each other with curiosity as we eased toward the door to investigate.

The same panther from last night had returned and was in his playful mood again. "This is mighty strange. It's got to be a trick. He's *trying* to lure us outside." Mrs. Brady shook her head as she spoke.

"Should I call Layne? I really would like for him to see this," I suggested as I watched the playful kitty. My intuition told me there was more to his actions than what we witnessed. This was not a trick, and he had something important he wanted to tell us.

The cat left his location at the back door rolling in the grass, playfully pawing the air, and meandered over to the clothesline where Mrs. Brady's last load of laundry for the day hung to dry. A slow glance back toward the door and he turned to tug at a pair of overalls.

"Give me my shotgun! That cussed cat is going to ruin my clean clothes," Mrs. Brady had grabbed the double-barrel and was tearing at the lock on the door when the cat ripped a pair of overalls from the line and disappeared behind the old pick-up truck parked in the yard. "Dad gum it, he's a dead cat now!"

Before either of us could stop her, Mrs. Brady had reached the door at the edge of the porch and proceeded out into the yard. A young man dressed only in a freshly washed, air-dried pair of denim overalls stepped out from behind the truck. He wore a bashful expression, and his hands were shoved deep into the pockets.

"Where'd you come from? And why are you stealing folk's clothes?" Mrs. Brady held fast to the shotgun pointed in his direction and waited for answers to her questions.

"I'm sorry, Ma'am. It would have been disrespectful not to mention downright embarrassing to show myself without clothes. I'd like to talk to you all, inside, if you don't mind." He nodded toward the house and waited for an invitation, but a sense of urgency and uneasiness radiated in his voice accompanied by a similar facial expression. He kept an eye on the three of us but glanced back over his shoulders one at a time.

"Who are you, boy? I don't recognize you as one of Tom's people. How do we know we can trust you?" Mr. Brady had stepped in front of his womenfolk and took a protective stance.

"I'm not part of Tom's clan, sir, not anymore. I'm sure he wouldn't have me back now anyway." He hung his head and exhaled a quick breath before he continued. "My name is Daniel Weaver. Folks call me Boone. I'm Del's son, and I need your help."

"Boone Weaver?" I eased out from behind my guardian and protector to get a better view of the young man. "You pumped gas at Lancaster's Service Station in Cranford six or seven years ago, didn't you?" I recognized something familiar about this boy. My Granddaddy Lancaster hired teenagers to help around the store from time to time. Boone was one of them—a good boy, and a hard worker. He never caused any trouble and was one of the best employees Granddaddy ever had. He could depend on Boone to do a job and do it right. Granddaddy was always a good judge of character, and I trusted his judgment even to this day.

"Yes, Ma'am, Ms. Lynzi. I hoped you'd remember me." Relief covered his face. He smiled for the first time as if, at long last, he had found a port in a storm.

The blood-curdling scream of a massive panther broke the through the still of the night and startled us all. Boone seemed the most frightened. My heart went out to this boy. Although he himself was a panther, he seemed genuinely afraid of what might be lurking in the dark.

I turned to the Bradys. "I think we can trust him. He truly seems to need our help. It's just a feeling but if I'm half the judge of character Granddaddy was, Boone's telling the truth. He *does* need our help." I held my breath and searched their eyes for their acknowledgement.

Mr. Brady appeared to be pondering all he'd heard for a moment before he gave his nod of agreement. Mrs. Brady was skeptical but stepped aside and said, "Come on in, but I'm keeping this shotgun handy in case this is a trick of some kind."

I took Boone's hand and led him inside the house. He stood stock still by the door after we were locked safe and sound inside and blew out a relieved breath. He shoved his hands back into his pockets and lowered his head, his gaze fixed on the floor.

Mrs. Brady was still on high alert and held the shotgun on him from her position by the kitchen sink.

Boone glanced in her direction. "I can't blame you one bit for wanting to be careful, Ma'am. But to tell you the truth, I'd rather you shoot me dead right here and now than to have to go along with that man another minute. There's no hope for him. He's . . . crazy." Tears filled Boone's eyes as he hung his head again.

My chest squeezed tight at the thought of everything this boy had endured in his short life. "You poor thing. Come sit down and tell us all about it. Are you hungry? Let me fix you a sandwich." I took some leftover chicken from the refrigerator and grabbed a loaf of bread. Placing the food on the table, I turned to retrieve a plate. I didn't have time to warm the chicken in the microwave or put any between slices of bread.

Obviously half starved, Boone dug right in. Before I could get the milk and a glass, he had deboned two entire chicken halves and gone through almost a half loaf of bread. I stood with my mouth open and watched as he devoured the leftovers. "Oh my, you *were* hungry." I set the glass and pitcher of milk on the table and took a seat across from him.

His face turned three shades of red from embarrassment as he stopped and wipe his mouth on the back of his hand. "I'm sorry. I'm acting like a pig. I do have manners. It's just . . . I-I haven't eaten in a couple of days."

"What's the matter, boy? Thousands of pounds of fresh beef not good enough for you?"

I knew that Mr. Brady was still sick over the senseless loss of all the livestock, and he verbalized his frustration loud and clear.

"Mr. Brady, you folks have no reason at all to believe me, but I never killed a single cow. Not one. I did feed off some of the kills, but only to survive. Del has been drugging Jesse and me for years to control us and have us do whatever he wanted. Robbing, stealing . . . it's just not right. I couldn't take it anymore." Boone closed his eyes as if to shut off the memory. "I let him think I took the pills, but I always tossed them out when he turned around. Then he came up with the idea to run you folks out and take over here and I had to try to do something. I came along to keep an eye on him and find out all his plans." He paused and directed his attention toward me.

"Then I saw Ms. Lynzi in the pasture yesterday and prayed she would help me. The Lancaster's were good to me when I worked for them. I ran away from Del when I was fifteen and came back here. Mr. Lancaster gave me a job at the service station. He thought the whole family had all moved back out here and I let him believe it." He lowered his head again. "I'm sorry I lied to your granddaddy, Ms. Lynzi, but I had to. I was afraid he would turn me in as a runaway and the sheriff would make me go back to Del. I was sleeping in the woods, living off the land, bathing, and washing my clothes in the creek. I saved up and bought a used car from him. That old car was my home until Del found me and dragged me back." He sniffled and sucked in another breath before he continued. "He took all the money I had saved away from me and shoved more pills down my throat to bring me back under his control. I was out of it for a few years. Hooked on the pills. But I stopped. I've just been going along with him until I could find another chance to run away."

He drained a second glass of milk before he continued. "I recognized you yesterday morning walking out in the pasture. I remember how kind you were to me back then, same as your granddaddy. I wanted a chance to explain and ask for your help to be free of Del. I want a chance to save my brother, too." His head dropped into his hands. The poor boy was exhausted. Tired of living a bad life. He had a good heart and needed our help to prove it.

Mrs. Brady stood the old shotgun in the corner and with her husband, eased into chairs at the table with Boone and me. They exchanged a long glance as if silently communicating with each other before Mr. Brady spoke. "Of course we'll help you. It takes a big man to come forward like you did. You're safe here now. We'll see to it. There's a room for you upstairs. You finish eatin' and get some rest. We'll talk more in the mornin'."

"Thank you. Thank you all. You're good people." The weight of the world seemed to have been lifted off his shoulders. He raised his head and smiled through the tears that threatened to spill from his eyes.

Mrs. Brady offered him a napkin, stroked his hair, and patted him on the back. "I'll go get your room ready. Layne has extra clothes here. You're about the same size. I'll leave some out on your bed and make sure there are towels in the bathroom." Her brow knit together as she raised her head and focused on something behind me.

Boone stared in the same direction with a terrified expression. His chair fell to the floor with a thud as he jerked upright and backed away from the table. Mr. Brady jumped to his feet as I turned to find a more than concerned Layne Brady standing behind me.

Before I could open my mouth to fill him in on the new development, he hooked one arm around my waist, hoisted me from my chair, and held me at his side like a rag doll. "What's *he* doing here?" Layne demanded. The veins protruded from his neck. His voice was enraged. I had not heard that degree of anger from him since Allvis kidnapped me a few weeks ago.

Squirming and wiggling, I began to address the situation. "Layne Brady, put me down! What is the matter with you? Have you lost your mind?"

"That's one of them, Lynzi. How did he get in here?" Layne extended his free arm, pointed to Boone, and waited for his questions to be answered.

"Well, if you'd stop treating me like a sack of potatoes and put me down, I'd tell you! Mercy!" I crossed my arms over my chest and waited for my words to sink into that stubborn head of his.

Everyone held their positions until the heat subsided a degree or two and Layne decided it was safe enough to put me down which meant for a moment, I was stuck with my feet dangling in the air. He eased my feet to the floor and slid me behind him, placing his body between Boone and me in a protective position.

"Layne, we heard him out. We believe his story, son." Mr. Brady stepped toward us and placed a reassuring hand on his son's shoulder.

I stepped around him and eased my palm against his cheek, drawing his attention. "Layne, I remember Boone. He worked for Granddaddy Lancaster at the service station several years back after he ran away from Del and tried to make a life on his own."

It took a moment for him to absorb my words before his shoulders relaxed a bit and he started to inhale regular breaths again. Everyone settled back at the table and related the story for a second time before the Bradys took Boone to his room to get cleaned up and get some rest. Layne and I sat for a time in silence and stared into our coffee mugs.

"My heart goes out to that poor boy. He was always the sweetest, most helpful young man . . . polite, and well mannered. Any parent would be proud and honored to have a son like Boone. But to think how he was abused and *drugged* by his own father makes me *sick*." I spit out the words. My hands covered my face and moisture collected in my eyes at the thought of the horrors Boone and his brother had suffered.

Layne blew out a breath, eased me onto his lap, and cradled my head to his chest. "I'm sorry, sweetheart," he said with a sigh. "I smelled panther and cattle blood and all I could think was *trap*."

"I understand, sweetie, and I don't blame you one bit. I want you to be safe, too." I squeezed my eyes shut and tried to ease my fears.

"I will never forget the abuse Del dished out to those boys. They were a few years younger than me, so I didn't hang out with them but when my friends and I went swimming down at the creek they'd be playing there. I saw the marks across their backs. New ones, old ones, I couldn't imagine what happened. My friends told me their daddy got drunk and beat them. I should have known he would never stop, that things would only get worse as time went on, but giving children *drugs* to control them." He huffed out an exasperated breath and shook his head.

"I hate Del for what he's done as much as you do. No one was able to help Boone before, but we *can* save him now and his brother, too."

"You're right. My beautiful, levelheaded, Lynzi. What would I do without you?" He wrapped his arms tighter around me and pressed his lips to my forehead before bringing us eye to eye. "He has to be stopped. We need to go find Tom. You up for a trip out in the woods?"

I nodded and closed my eyes as Layne positioned me for our quick trip outside.

8

"Funny, this doesn't look anything like the woods," I said as I opened my eyes to the sight of the hayloft and one of Layne's *gotcha* grins.

"I thought a stop in the hayloft might be a nice place for a . . . talk." He tugged me into his arms and rubbed his cheek against the top of my head, humming his satisfaction of being alone or maybe that he had pulled one over on me again, but I suspected it was a combination of the two.

"Uh-oh. I thought we settled this in the kitchen. One of your *talks* usually means I'm about to get scolded about keeping myself safe and—" He took my chin between his thumb and a crooked forefinger and lifted my head to bring our lips together for one of his all-consuming, weak in the knees kisses. His sure-fire method of bringing about an end to anything I was saying or thinking at the time. His lips left mine but hovered over my mouth before he kissed each lip one at a time.

"Mmm, scold me again," I breathed, tugging his bottom lip between mine.

He closed his eyes and inhaled a deep cleansing breath. "I don't intend to scold you, my sweetheart. I *may* have overreacted a *tiny* bit in the kitchen earlier, but I do trust your judgment and now that more of the pieces to this insane puzzle are in place, we can begin to plan our next move. Del will find out soon enough Boone is missing and figure we captured or

61

killed him. We've got to get everyone together for a meeting, but, as long as we're here . . ." He grinned as he slipped my shirt over my head and tossed it onto the hay. My heart rate sped to a healthy thump.

My eyes went wide. Amazed Layne would begin to disrobe me here in the barn where anyone could walk in. "Layne, what if Lake or one of the boys pops in? Where is Woods anyway? Isn't this *his* post?" I put up a slight protest even though I was certain he had that situation along with the hooks at the back of my bra well in hand.

"I sent Woods to the barn at our place. They all know how serious this situation is and would never abandon their posts. If they need me, they'll call. I've alerted my teams of some new developments, and they will meet us in the kitchen for breakfast. So, we are all alone here." He stepped closer as he lowered me to the hay bed. Now, how did the quilt from our bed get here in the hayloft? Hmm.

He knelt at my side and gazed at me with loving eyes. Moonlight spilled in through the door of the hayloft and illuminated his face. The face of my hero. My life. Layne's fingers brushed a stray strand of hair from my face as he studied me with care. "I can't wait for you to finally be my wife."

"Mmm, it won't be much longer. Mama and Aunt Pet have been in touch with Cloi and they're all working on the plans." I reached up and unbuttoned his shirt, slid it down to free his arms, and flicked it over my shoulder to keep company with my own.

Layne eased down beside me and rested on one elbow. Taking my wrists in his free hand, he raised my arms above my head. "Mmm, you enticing woman." His voice was soft and low.

His gaze swept the entire length of my body before he lowered his head to bring our lips together.

First time sensations sizzled through every nerve ending each time we made love. His touch new, yet familiar and always left me breathless. He never went mechanically through the motions. He studied me with his own anticipation, his eyes danced with pleasure from my reactions.

Our slow rhythmic moves intensified as bolts of pleasure zinged through our bodies. We relaxed into an entwined position in the hay. Layne tucked me under his chin as he whispered, "I can't get enough of you. You are my life, Lynzi. Without you, I don't know how I would have survived all this time. You kept me alive. You were so strong to go on with your life after I left you. Thank you for keeping me safe in the corner of your heart. You are my world."

"The past made us both what we are today. Now we're together in the present and we have forever to look forward to. Our lives are perfect, and we only have more good times ahead." I snuggled down as he drew the quilt up to cocoon us for the night.

I opened my eyes as Layne stirred several hours later. "What's wrong?" I asked, realizing he was communicating with another Fae.

"Lake has spotted a couple of cats moving in the woods behind his house. He's pretty sure it's Del and one of his boys but he'd like my opinion. I'm sorry, darlin', I'll only be a hot minute." He winked as he tucked the quilt close around me.

"The hot part I believe. Don't be too long. I'll miss you." I snuggled down in my hay bed with lovemaking aftershocks still sending sparks through my body.

"Stay under the covers, I'll be back in a jiffy," Layne kissed my temple as he whisked off to his panther identification consultation with Lake.

Mmm, I thought, why do people spend hundreds or thousands of dollars on bedding sets when a good old-fashioned hay bed was every bit as *comfortable.* I curled into a ball and drew the guilt closer to keep warm since my heat source had left me for the moment, but a loud bang on the barn door below startled me to a sitting position.

Was Layne back so soon? No, I thought, if he were, he would be here beside me not outside causing a commotion that would bring unwanted attention to us. Someone else is here. I scrambled for my clothes and yanked on my jeans and T-shirt in a flash.

Inching my way quietly down the ladder to the ground floor of the barn with extreme care, I listened and watched for any movement as I descended. No additional sounds had been made. Maybe it was only one of the farm animals moving about in the predawn hours. I tried to reassure myself, easing closer to the entrance for a better view when an upright shadow passed in front of the door and stopped. That's not a farm animal. I searched the area around me for something to protect myself with if need be. The pitchfork in the tool rack became my best friend at that moment. I armed myself in the event I needed to defend my territory including my life.

The door creaked open and revealed a tall man with a weathered face, one old before his time resulting from hard living, and no care for his health.

"Who are you and what are you doing here?" I demanded. I raised the pitchfork with the sharp tines directed toward his chest, my feet planted in a defensive stance, a white-knuckled grip on the handle. I had made the acquaintance of all the neighbors in the area and this man didn't fall into the *neighbor* category. Anyway, none of them would be prowling around on other folk's property in the wee hours before dawn.

"Well, well. Who are you, missy? I don't remember there being any Brady girls. You're a mighty pretty young thing, though." He took another step toward me, a disgusting smirk smeared across his face.

My heart pounded in my chest, but I couldn't allow the fear swelling inside me to show on my face. I had to maintain a confident air. I drew in steady, even breaths.

He took another step toward me. "Stay back! I'll ask again. Who *are* you?" I kept the pitchfork pointed in his direction to let him know I would use it if push came to shove. I had been armed with a shotgun on our hunting trip a few weeks ago and I'd sure be more confident with it in my hands right about now, but given the situation, I had to make do with what I had available.

"Now, wait a minute, missy. You don't have no reason to be afraid of me. I'm an old friend of Will Brady's. I used to live around here a while back and decided to move home again. The name's Weaver, Del Weaver." He took another step toward me with an expression I was sure he intended to be friendly, but it didn't come off as such to me. He reeked of plain old meanness, not to mention stale whiskey.

"Stay back! I know *exactly* who you are, and I also know you don't deserve to walk the face of this earth after the way you abused your boys all their lives. You're a despicable excuse for a father and human being." A surge of disgust flared inside me, I could have shoved the tines of the old fork through his chest and not batted an eye. No one should be allowed to live after abusing children!

He snarled and bared his grubby brown teeth. "Humpf. I'll show you who won't be walkin' the earth, you uppity female," Del blurted out as he lunged toward me.

I held firm to the handle of the pitchfork intent on making my mark on his sorry hide and braced myself for the impact. A split second before contact was made, I sensed an invisible arm latch onto my waist from behind and the tingle of teleportation begin. Layne had returned at the exact moment of Del's attack to rescue me.

"Hell fire, another damn witch! I'll kill you, too, you bitch!" Del raised a fist and screamed out his threat as I faded from the barn.

My feet settled on the kitchen floor of the Brady house, still holding fast to the pitchfork.

"Stay here!" Layne shouted his order as he disappeared again.

"Wait! Don't go back. He might see you." I feared Del would tell all the wrong people Layne was still alive if he found out. I waited a few seconds, half expecting him to reappear. Nothing. "Why can't you listen to *me* for once? I worry about you, too." I found myself pleading into thin air. Should I get the shotgun and go after him myself? Probably not a good idea since he could be anywhere by now, I debated with myself. I needed to help fix this *and* protect Layne.

"Lynzi? Honey? Why are you worried about the pitchfork . . . in the kitchen?" Mrs. Brady's concern was loud and clear, but her tone was soft and low. I turned wide-eyed to the pair who had made their way down the stairs with expressions of utter confusion. They watched as I appeared to hold a one-sided conversation with a pitchfork in the middle of their kitchen.

"Oh. Oh my." My gaze switched from the Brady's confused faces to the pitchfork in my hand and back again. "You, you must think I've lost my mind. I wasn't speaking to this," I indicated the tool in my right hand. I relayed the story of my earlier encounter with Del while Mrs. Brady put on a pot of coffee.

"So, he thinks you disappeared from the barn under your own power and that must make you a witch. This complicates matters I'm afraid. You're going to be in danger too, now that he sees you as a threat," Layne's daddy summed up the latest development.

"My thoughts exactly, Daddy." Layne had reappeared by the door.

I propped the pitchfork against the refrigerator and extended both hands to hold off the anticipated *putting yourself in danger* lecture. "Layne, before you say anything, I didn't stay in the loft like you said, but if I *had* I would've been cornered without *any* way to defend myself if Del had come up the ladder."

Layne's expression softened. He folded both my hands in his and brought them to his lips. "Hush now, sweetheart. None of that was your fault. You did the only thing you could do to try to defend yourself. And a very effective weapon of choice by the way." Layne nodded toward the lone defender now propped by the fridge as he wrapped me in his protective arms and rocked us while he shushed my fears. "Shh, hush now, darlin'. Everything's gonna be okay."

Now that I was safe and wrapped in his arms again, the realization of the danger I had been in caused me to shake. "Del thinks I'm a witch and said he's going to kill me, too." Not that I was worried he would ever get close enough to me again to follow through with his threat. There were many guardians in many forms all around me. Still, the threat had been uttered and now added to our dilemma.

"And that was all the confession I needed to hear to be sure he killed Ellen. But, as far as him getting anywhere near you again, that *will not* happen."

The shaking started all over again. I had made yet another enemy who meant to do me harm.

Layne stroked my hair and whispered soothing words in my ear. The combination of the sound of his voice and the warm breath bathing my neck eased my fears and calmed my frazzled nerves.

Mr. Brady sat with his hands folded on the table in front of him studying the checked pattern on the tablecloth. "Tom should be here for breakfast soon. We'll tell him Del's been prowling around the barn in human form as well as animal. I'm not so sure you and the boys should hold back now, Layne. It's bad enough that he's intent on putting us out of business by killing off all our stock but Del made this personal when he threatened Lynzi."

He swiped a hand over his face and huffed out a breath. "This can't get any more serious. Not when my daughter has been threatened. Tom's folks need to find some way to mark themselves, put on a red collar or a cowbell, some way they can be identified when they're in cat form 'cause I intend to start shooting all unmarked cats on sight. I won't stand by and have my womenfolk afraid to step foot outside on our own land, dad blame it!" Mr. Brady pounded his fist on the table to punctuate his intent.

"Yes Sir, Daddy. I agree. We can't allow this to go on." Layne's frustration and determination echoed his daddy's.

"Coffee's ready," Mrs. Brady sang out as she slid a tray with mugs and the coffee pot on the table and placed her hand on Mr. Brady's shoulder. "We'll figure this all out Will," she whispered. Her hand adjusted a fold in his collar.

I moved my forked weapon to the corner by the door and retrieved the cream pitcher from the fridge. Events of the morning rebounded through my thoughts. Boone's voice drew my attention to the doorway.

"I didn't mean to eavesdrop folks, but I overheard what happened in the barn. Ms. Lynzi, are you sure you're okay? I'm sorry if I've made things harder on everybody by coming to you for help. I wouldn't do anything to hurt you for the world." Boone stood back. Fear and frustration in his eyes. Like a lost, little boy. As if we were about to blame him for his father's despicable actions.

"Of course you wouldn't, Boone. You come on in and sit down with the family now. The coffee's ready and Mrs. Brady and I are about to start breakfast." I took his hand and led him to the table.

"As far as we know now, Del doesn't even know you're here. But he will soon enough, and we need to have all the facts so we can make a plan." Layne poured the coffee and passed the cream pitcher around the table as he explained his dual life, his Fae abilities, and why Del now thinks, I'm a witch.

He continued. "This is something we have to keep quiet. My folks could get into big trouble for helping fake my death and concealing the truth all these years."

"Layne, you folks have shown me more kindness in the past eight hours than I've known in years. I'll help you any way I can, and your secret will go to my grave with me. I swear it." The fear and uncertainty had eased somewhat from Boone's face, and he became more at ease as pancakes and sausages were being served.

"Boone, Mrs. Brady and I talked about this last night, and we decided you have a home here with us for as long as you like. And there's the possibility Tom may invite you back to the clan, but whatever you decide to do, just know you're always welcomed here." Mr. Brady extended his offer of a home as he passed the sausages.

A tear threatened to spill from the boy's eye as he fought to speak. "I appreciate the offer. I would love to stay here with you all. I want to work the farm for you and try to repay at least some of what's been taken from you. I-I can't believe y'all can accept me so easy after what I was a part of."

"You mean what you were *forced* to be a part of. You have a family now, Boone. And a true family takes care of its own." This boy was special with a good heart and the way he had been treated ripped a hole in my chest. He deserved a chance to be happy.

The panes rattled in the door as Tom and Lake along with two ravenous guard teams filed into the kitchen. From his surprised expression, Tom picked up the scent of a strange panther right away and paused to evaluate the situation. He hadn't seen Boone in years. His body stiffened, assessing the situation he had walked in on.

I took my position at Boone's side and placed a hand on his shoulder for support. Tom had to see he was no threat.

"Come on in and sit down, Tom. This is Boone Weaver. We've heard him out. He wants to help us rid ourselves of Del and his meanness. He's never been a part of Del's plan here." To avoid any misunderstandings Mr. Brady relayed the events of last evening and this morning.

Tom sat quietly. His chin propped on doubled fists, listening as Mr. Brady spoke, and paused before speaking himself, pressing for more details. "Boone if you want to rejoin the clan, I'd be proud to have you back. I know now none of this was your doing. What can you tell us about your mama? How did she die?"

Boone swallowed hard. Tears welled up in his eyes and he lowered his gaze to the table.

"Take your time." Tom appeared genuinely concerned for the boy as well as putting an end to the misery Del had caused.

Boone sucked in a sharp breath and let it ease out before he began. "Thank you, Tom, but the Bradys have offered to let me stay here for a while. I'd like to stay and work on the farm to try and pay them back for at least some of their loss. As for my mama—"

This was bound to be a difficult subject for him to rehash. I stepped to the table with another platter of sausages. "Why don't we all eat our breakfast before it gets cold and then we can talk?" I directed my gaze to Tom with a raised brow indicating my question was actually a firm request. Tom picked right up on this and nodded his agreement. This couldn't be an easy story for poor Boone to relive and I wanted to get some food in him first. At least for a few minutes he could focus on something other than the memories of his mother's death.

9

"My mama was a good woman. She laughed and played games with me and Jesse, and never got tired. She'd run and hunt with us at night all by herself since Del was almost always gone." Boone became quiet. His eyes softened and a slight smile slipped over his lips. At least he had a few good memories of his mama left. But that smile faded as he continued. "But she was forever looking around the next corner for him. Waiting for him to come home and be what she wanted him to be. She made bad choice after bad choice. All of 'em on account of him." Boone's features softened when he spoke of his mother but that pleasant expression faded when Del's name passed his lips.

"When Del left our cabin in the woods down the road here, Mama packed everything she could into that old station wagon, and we took off after him. She talked about how much better our life would be and how much fun we'd have campin' and huntin' when we found him, and he took his *medicine*. That's what she called it. That stuff Granny made was supposed to bring out the good side of him and make him the kind of man Mama wanted him to be, a good husband and father." He huffed out a short breath and shook his head. "But it didn't work. I reckon because he didn't have a good side to bring out. He still beat all of us, every chance he got. It was his idea of home life." He paused and blinked away the moisture that had formed in his eyes.

I eased a glass of water onto the table next to Boone's plate. This couldn't be easy for him to remember and carry around with him every day much less speak it out loud to a room full of strangers.

Boone paused and took a couple of sips from his glass before he continued. "She always said it would only be a few more days, then things would be better. Just a few more days, she'd say. But he'd get drunk and call us all together. He made me and Jesse watch while he beat her with his belt. And when we cried, or tried to stop him, he'd turn the belt on us." He puffed out his chest and shook his head with a scowl, mocking Del. "*I'm teaching you boys how to be real men and keep your woman under control,* he'd say."

Boone drew in a labored breath and pushed forward with his story. "One day he beat her so bad she fell and didn't get up. Never moved again. She was *dead*. He made a laughing sound like she had done something bad by dying, called her a weak female. He turned up the bottle he was working on and took a long drink, then made me and Jesse wrap her up in a bed sheet, drag her out in the backyard, and dig a hole to bury her."

He squeezed his eyes shut, then sniffled, and swiped at his nose with his hand. A disgusted look spread across his face. He gritted his teeth. "He stood there popping open beer after beer and yelling at us to dig harder. We dug a hole best we could with sticks and old boards. He pushed her over the edge with his foot and made us cover her up. Then he . . . I'm sorry, Mama. I'm so sorry I didn't save you." Boone covered his face with his hands to hide the tears.

His sobs tore at my heart. My entire body as well as my voice shook. "That's enough. He's been through enough. You know what happened now. Leave him alone." I choked out the words. No good would come of any more detail and I wasn't about to stand by and watch this boy torment himself a second longer. "It's okay, Boone, you don't have to say anything else. We get the picture." My voice broke as I fought back tears of my own.

I placed a hand on his shoulder, not sure how he would receive being comforted by me in a room full of men. I needed to pull the little boy part of him onto my lap and rock him until he cried it out, to tell him everything would be okay, and that I would protect him from Del, but a full-grown man sat at the table, and I had to remember to treat him like a man.

I glanced around the table to the faces of Lake and the guard team. I had witnessed these men on the battlefield, wielding swords, and slaying the thugs who followed Allvis. These men were fierce and brave, but all were on the verge of tears themselves after hearing the horrors Boone, his brother, and their mother had endured.

"You're right, Lynzi." Tom shook his head. Guilt covered his face. His own eyes glistened with moisture. He had said before, if he'd acted years ago, he could have prevented all the misery Ellen and the boys had suffered. I could tell he blamed himself. "We've suspected it all along but now, we have all the proof we need. My hunters will wear red bandanas around their necks tonight. Everyone else in the clan will stay in human form. I am even more determined now to bring Del in. Not to make an example of him to any of my clan but to right a mistake *I* made years ago. I fully understand you folks doing anything necessary to protect your loved ones, but I still want him alive. He must face his crimes."

"What about Jesse? Can I try to find him and talk to him? I couldn't save Mama but maybe I can save my brother." Boone's face was still stained with tears, but he had come from his dark place and rejoined the planning session.

"Boone, you're a grown man. I'm not saying you have to sit this one out but Del must have found out you're gone by now. If he runs across you, he'll likely turn on you. Why don't you let us handle it? We'll bring Jesse to you." Layne's protective side expanded to include Boone now as well.

"I can't sit by and do nothing. I need to at least help even if I can't end this myself." Boone sounded more determined now to be a part of the solution.

"He may be able to spot something we've missed, Layne. If he's in the hayloft at my place with us it should be safe enough." Lake to the rescue. I could always depend on him in a pinch. I smiled and mouthed the words, "thank you" to him in appreciation. He winked and nodded his acknowledgement.

After breakfast, Tom, Lake, and the guards went their separate way to get some much-needed sleep. They had to be refreshed and alert for another nightlong watch to protect the remaining livestock.

When the dishes were done, we all sat around the table and enjoyed more coffee. Not wanting to desert Boone on his first full day here, Layne and I decided to hang out with him. It sure wasn't safe for any of us to be outside.

"Get the cards, gal." Mr. Brady's idea of a family game was just what we needed. The five of us played rummy at the kitchen table.

Boone was uneasy at first but as we laughed and talked about life here and back at the ranch, he became more relaxed and joined in the conversation and family fun.

"I forgot how good it feels to laugh. Feel safe. Be with good people." Boone glanced out the door. It didn't take a mind reader to figure out what he was thinking. His brother was out there, somewhere, and he wanted to save him from Del's continued bad influence.

By late afternoon, Mr. Brady decided it was time to refill the hay rings for the cows one last time until this springs pasture grass filled in completely.

"I'd like to help you Daddy but if hay bales start floating across the pasture, folks might start to talk." Layne had told me time and time again how he hated not being able to take a more active part in the work his daddy had to do on the farm. "I'm afraid Boone still shouldn't go outside at this point either."

"Don't worry, son. I've been doing this for more years than I care to remember. I won't be long." Mr. Brady reached for his crumpled old John Deere cap on the hook by the door.

"I'll go with you. Mrs. Brady is taking a nap before time to fix supper. I'm not much muscle but I loved going to the pasture to check on the cows with Granddaddy when I was a little girl."

"All right then gal, grab your hat. I'd enjoy your company." Mr. Brady's eyes lit up as he accepted my offer of help.

I gave Layne a quick peck on the cheek and grabbed one of his old baseball caps from the rack. Some father daughter bonding time would be fun.

We climbed up into the cab of the big tractor and selected a fresh round bale to take out to the cows. The short distance to the metal holding ring used to keep the hay somewhat intact as the cows fed was covered in a quick minute. We sat for another few minutes to take a head count and observe the cows to make sure we saw no injuries or visible ailments in need of tending. Several of the cows had given birth earlier in the spring and called to their calves to keep close.

"Uh-oh. Check out the calf coming up the path." I noticed one struggling to keep up with the others. We stepped down from our perch on the tractor to investigate closer. I prayed it would be an easy fix and as we approached, we noticed something was tangled around the poor things back foot. Fishing line, probably snagged, and broken in the edge of the pond had become wrapped tight around his lower leg and cut into his skin.

"I'll hold him still, gal, you cut the line from his foot." Mr. Brady handed his pocketknife over for me to use to free the calf's foot.

The little fella was well behaved and allowed me to complete the task with only a couple of cuts to the tangled line. A splash of peroxide from the first aid box on board the tractor and the baby scampered off to join his mother.

"You caught that just in time, gal. If both his feet had got tangled together, he wouldn't be able to walk. A calf down is an invitation for predators and Lord knows we've had more than our share of those lately." He gave me a pat on the back as we turned toward the tractor.

"Speak of the devil," Mr. Brady said with a high level of aggravation imbedded in his words.

I followed his stare to a man propped against the tractor. Del Weaver.

"Well, well. Will Brady. Fancy seeing you here. And what a pretty little sidekick you got with you. What'd you do, trade in the old lady for a newer model? Ain't nothin' wrong with gettin' some new tail ever now and then. No, sir, nothing at all." He laughed as if he had said something funny and expected us to join in.

"Shut your filthy mouth, Weaver, and get away from my tractor!" Mr. Brady started for the opposite side of the cab. I figured he wanted to get the rifle from behind the seat. It was kept there to take care of varmints being a bother around the farm and Del Weaver certainly fell into that category.

"You lookin' for this, old man?" Del smirked as he brought the rifle into sight and pointed it at Mr. Brady. "You come on over here now, old man. Me and you need to have a talk, then me and the little lady there can get better acquainted." Another smirk. This one turned my stomach. I searched the ground for something to defend myself with. My fingers tightened their grip on the pocketknife still in my hand. I kept a close eye on Del and the rifle he held gauging the situation and weighing my options.

Mr. Brady made his way around the front of the tractor. Del drew back and jabbed the barrel of the rifle hard into Mr. Brady's side causing him to double over in pain.

"Leave him alone, Del!" I shrieked as I reached inside the collar of my shirt and rubbed my pendant between my thumb and forefinger. Aunt Pet had given me a silver pendant with a special, magical charge that would call Layne to my side whenever I needed him.

Del hooked his arm around Mr. Brady's neck and pointed the rifle at me. "Shut your mouth and be patient, witch, I'll get to you in due time. In due time."

A warm hand pressed into my lower back. "I'm here, darlin'," Layne whispered low in my ear.

I tried to muffle my voice so we wouldn't be discovered. "Layne, you have to help Daddy. He's hurt bad."

"I will, darlin'. First, I need you to bring out your best lynx attitude right now. Raise your hand real slow and point to Del. Tell him you're only going to say once more to let Daddy go. I'll take care of the rest. Trust me." Layne had a plan and from his amused tone he was gonna enjoy every minute of it.

"I trust you with my life." I focused on the pure evil standing before us, raised my arm in a slow, determined fashion, and pointed a stiffened finger straight at him.

"What are you mumbling about over there, witch? You talking some kinda magic mumbo jumbo? Ha!" Del tightened his grip as he continued laughing.

"This is your last warning, Del. Let go of him. Now!" The wind began to stir and the hideous smirk that had spread from ear to ear slowly faded.

"You don't scare me, witch. You ain't got no control over the wind." He gawked back and forth, studying the mini tornado swirling around us. He adjusted his arm around Mr. Brady's neck. "You, you don't scare me."

The wind whipped harder as it stirred up debris and scattered twigs and leaves around.

"Hold on, sweetheart. I'm about to make a believer out of him," Layne whispered in my ear.

I held my position. My eyes were fixed in a determined stare, and I kept my finger pointed at Del as Layne brought on more wind along with a few rocks. One of the heavier ones happened to smack Del upside the head, hard enough to bring him to his knees.

Del loosened his hold on Mr. Brady as the two of them collapsed to the ground. The rifle stock slammed into the dirt and a shot discharged with a loud crack that echoed off the wood line. More rocks pounded Del's back. This assault encouraged him to scramble to his feet and run like heck for the woods. "I'll get you! I'll get you both!" He yelped as he ran off, the whirlwind followed him to the edge of the woods, rocks continuing to pound him relentlessly.

I hurried to Mr. Brady's side. The impact of the rifle barrel in his side must have cracked some ribs I figured since it was difficult for him to catch his breath. Every attempt to draw air into his lungs was short and labored.

Thoughts of getting Daddy to safety flooded my head. I kept one eye on the tree line, fully expecting Del to come charging out at us in panther form with intentions of ripping us both apart. "Layne, you need to get Daddy to the house now. I'll bring the tractor."

"I'm not leaving you out here alone, Lynzi." Layne had helped his daddy to his feet and hooked another arm around my waist.

I retrieved the rifle from the dirt and held it up. "I'll be fine. I'll be there in two minutes. Now go. Call Aunt Pet to meet you at the house." For once, my words penetrated that stubborn, protective head of his and he listened to *me*. He loosened his hold on me, and the two of them faded from sight.

I climbed into the cab, started the engine, and hauled butt back to the house. My heart was racing a mile a minute as I bypassed the barn and skidded to a stop at the back door. Mrs. Brady stood guard outside, shotgun in hand to cover me as I made my way into the house in case Del had doubled back and was lurking, waiting to carry out his latest threat.

"How is he?" I was worried but tried my best to keep up a brave front. Layne's daddy was a kind and gentle man and didn't deserve anything else in return.

"Pet is with him now. He's working on his second bottle of her herb tea and cussin' up a storm. Blames himself. Says *he* should have taken care of Del," she said.

"There was nothing he *could* do. Del caught us with our backs turned and took full advantage of the situation." I glanced back over my shoulder to make sure we didn't have any unwanted company.

We joined everyone in the kitchen. Mr. Brady sure *sounded* stronger as he barked out new orders. "Nobody goes outside alone or unarmed until we settle this!"

"Tractor's outside. Here's the key. Are you sure you're okay?" I scanned the faces of Layne and Aunt Pet to gather any sign of concern although I had every confidence in Aunt Pet and her healing abilities. She had healed many other serious injuries, some of my own from time to time but still, I worried.

"Aw, it'll take more than a couple of cracked ribs to get me down. How 'bout you? You okay, Lynzi gal? I'm sorry you had to listen to that foul mouth of his. We'll get him, believe you me, we'll get him." If anything, Daddy was even more determined to put an end to Del and his devilment.

I prayed for that very ending myself. "I'm fine. You just drink your tea so those ribs will heal." I couldn't stand to see any of my family in pain.

Boone pointed to the floor; his brow wrinkled with worry. "Ms. Lynzi. You're bleeding."

10

I followed his stare to my foot and spotted a puddle of blood gathering on the floor. A steady drip fell from the hem of my jeans. The sight of blood streaming down my leg redirected my focus. The subsequent pain and fear hit and caused my knees to buckle. Confused as to how this happened, I grabbed the edge of the table to steady myself. My head began to swim, and my vision faded as black and white spots danced before my eyes.

"Lynzi, your leg!" Layne scooped me up in his arms and headed toward the couch where he examined the source of the blood. A hole in the left leg of my jeans revealed torn flesh. He slid my jeans off as Mama draped a lap quilt over me to provide some comfort from being more exposed than I cared to be in a room full of mixed company.

Aunt Pet and the others followed close behind. Her examination confirmed not one but two wounds, one on the front side of my left thigh, and one on the back directly behind the first.

"You have been shot, my little one. Here is the entry wound and there is the exit. The bullet went clean through your leg. But not to worry, we will have you good as new in no time at all." Aunt Pet sang out her diagnosis as she cleaned the wounds and applied some of her homemade healing salve to the .22 caliber holes in my leg.

Mr. Brady had finished his second bottle of herb tea and brought one for me. Aunt Pet's secret recipe of healing herbs and a dash of Fae magic helped to speed the healing process along and was always kept on hand for medical emergencies.

"Why didn't you tell me, sweetheart? You shouldn't have driven the tractor home in this condition." Layne cradled my head to his chest.

"I didn't have a clue myself until Boone pointed it out. I heard the rifle shot and I felt a thud hit my leg, but I thought it was a pebble from your miniature storm. Why do you suppose I didn't notice the pain until I saw the blood?" Thanks to the tea, my head had stopped spinning, my roiling tummy had settled, and the pain had subsided, somewhat.

"Your adrenaline had you focused on the situation with Daddy. I should never have allowed you to go outside. It's just too dangerous right now." Layne trembled as he held me close and tried to comfort me.

"It was my job to protect you. I should have kept you out of harm's way," Daddy said with more than a hint of guilt.

These men of mine, always ready to take blame for anything that goes wrong even when the situation was obviously out of their control. It was admirable but frustrating at the same time. "Would you two stop blaming yourselves? No one had any idea Del would show himself in broad open daylight. And Layne. *Allow?* Did you seriously just use the word, *allow?*"

He closed his eyes, hung his head, and laughed. "No ma'am, I . . . well, maybe it, *slipped* out."

I laughed despite the throbbing pain searing through my leg.

"Layne, we got trouble." Lake's voice came from the kitchen spiked with more concern than I had ever heard from him.

Lake and Woods rushed into the living room but stopped in their tracks when they spotted me on the couch and all the blood-soaked towels piled on the floor. "What happened? Lynzi? Are you okay?" Lake asked as they both skidded to a stop.

"Del shot her but thanks to Aunt Pet, she'll be fine." Layne answered Lake's questions but never took his eyes off me.

"That's more than I can say for that damned Del the next time I see him," Mr. Brady swore. His intention to stop Del had intensified with the incident this afternoon and everyone in the room fully understood that intent.

I worried he would do something dangerous like go after Del on his own.

"Del *shot* you? That psycho *shot* you?" Lake appeared stunned to say the least. He threw his hands up in the air as if he had heard it all now.

"Yeah. I'm told I'm lucky it went clean through and missed the bone. I suppose it could have been worse," I tried to sound brave through the burning discomfort, but the pain was winning at this point.

"You said there was more trouble. What kind, Lake? What's happened now?" Layne asked. We had had quite enough trouble for one day but now we were about to learn of more.

"I hate to tell y'all this now, but we found more dead cows. Fresh kills. It happened less than an hour ago maybe. Woods and I decided to make rounds before coming in for supper. We checked out my barn then went on to yours and found—" He paused as if to put off the bad news he had to share. "I'm sorry, Lynzi. We found all the calves in your barn . . . torn to shreds."

"Del must have gone straight to our barn when he ran from us in the pasture." Layne blew out an exasperated breath and shook his head.

"The calves I had set aside for the 4-H show? I had them locked away in the barn for safekeeping. That coward. He couldn't get the upper hand with us in the pasture, so he went and took out his frustrations on a bunch of helpless calves?" I attempted to push myself to a sitting position and gather the guilt around me to be able to stand without embarrassing everyone in the room, myself most of all.

A sea of hands flooded around me. Everyone reached out to keep me from standing. "Whoa, sweetheart, where do you think you're going?" Layne tried to keep me on the couch, but my leg beat us both to the punch.

I sank back to the most comfortable position possible with pain shooting from my wounds in every direction. I tried to make everyone believe that I was fine, but a groan slipped from my lips as I readjusted my body, panted to calm my roiling stomach, and to keep my lunch under control. I bit my bottom lip as I tried to conceal the pain.

"Layne, those calves were going to help the Miller kids down the road get started in the Young Farmers program so they could enter the calf show at the county fair this fall. The family moved here from the city to get a fresh start and raise the children in the safety of the country." I was sick. Sick that those poor little calves were dead and that if the Millers found out about all this, they might think no place on earth was safe enough to raise their family. I had begun the question the same fact myself.

"I know, honey, and we're gonna fix this before anybody finds out. I promise. You be still now and get your strength back. You have a certain *aisle* to walk down in a few days, remember?"

No argument from me on that one. I gave up even trying to move. Being shot and hearing that my sweet baby calves had been killed was a bit overwhelming to say the least. I tried to control myself, but the anger continued to build inside me.

"Everything's gonna be okay." Layne eased himself on the couch beside me and cuddled me in his arms.

The pain in my leg had subsided somewhat but the ache would keep me down for a couple of days at least. Even with Aunt Pet's salve and tea speeding the healing process, as a human, it always took longer to heal. We're not as fast as the Fae, who are natural healers.

Layne brushed the frazzled hair from my forehead and cupped my cheek as we shared a deep, loving glance. Our hearts connected and communicated with a fierce power when we shared these intense moments, making it hard to break away.

He inhaled sharply and turned his focus to Lake. "Send someone to find Tom. Make sure we have enough folks to put together a day watch as well as the cover the night. Tell him to put some of his guards at their posts around all the pastures and barns for the remainder of the day and we'll take over for them at dark. This is a twenty-four-hour watch now. Bring in another team from the ranch. Things have gone too far." Layne made eye contact with every person in the room as he spoke to confirm they understood his intentions.

Lake and Woods disappeared to carry out their assigned tasks. Aunt Pet busied herself handing out more tea to her patients and Mama did what Mama does best. She headed to the kitchen to start supper for the hungry crew on its way. We had an overabundance of fresh beef lately. Any that had not spoiled after they were killed went to the local butcher to be cut and packaged for the freezer. Tonight, we would feast on buttery cornbread and a pot of porcupine meatball stew. Meatballs made with rice that pokes out in all directions when it cooks.

"We need to get you upstairs and settled in bed for the night. I'll bring supper up to you." Layne raised his brow to get my approval of his nursing plan.

"As long as you promise to take a nap before supper. You have to go back on watch tonight and I want you alert in case Del tries something else. Or I should say *when* Del tries something else. He has proven his unpredictability, and I don't put anything past him now." I winced in pain as I tried to adjust to a more comfortable position.

"Now, darlin', you know I can't promise to sleep when I slide up next to you in bed." He grinned with that special twinkle dancing in his eyes.

I glanced at my bandaged leg and back to him with a little wrinkle of my nose.

"I know, baby." He exhaled an obvious fake sigh. "I'll just have to try harder to control myself. Hey, how 'bout you finish off that tea and I'll go get you another one." He leaned down for a quick kiss. Lightning flashes zinged through my body. How could one tiny kiss send so many pleasure sensations through me and bypass the pain from the holes in my leg?

Layne whisked me off to bed, brought my supper, made me comfortable, and tended to my every need. A quiet night followed. No disturbances. No dead cattle. It was as if Del wanted to confuse us. Take us by surprise. No incidents when we expected them then a shocker like the calves slaughtered in broad daylight. Unpredictable evil.

The ache in my leg had kept me awake most of the night. Pain accompanied by concern for Layne and the others. He had popped in to check on me several times during the night and provide updates. No rogue panthers wreaking havoc on any of the properties. Good news for sure but what was that devil up to next?

Shortly after the sun peeked through the window, he appeared with a breakfast tray in hand. "You should be asleep, sweetheart. Does your leg hurt? I brought more tea." My hero and protector eased into bed beside me.

I would be good as new in a couple of days with my magical medical treatments, but I needed to take it easy for the time being. I could get some rest now that Layne was back beside me and I was assured everyone was safe. "Are you going to get some sleep?"

"Yes, ma'am. As soon as you finish off your tea and we have a bite of this good breakfast Mama made for us." He poured cream into my coffee and traded the cup for my empty tea bottle. We chatted as we polished off the steak and eggs on our tray. "We can't get a handle on where that devil is hiding. Tom and his folks checked out all the places Boone suggested but they had been cleared out days ago. It's almost as if they have an inside line to what we're thinking and planning." Layne shook his head trying to figure this out.

It was as if someone was leaking information to Del but no way I'd ever believe Boone would double cross us. "Layne, I'm not Fae and I can't read hearts the same way you all are able to, but I am sure Boone's heart is honest and he would never betray us." I returned my empty cup to the tray and adjusted my position a bit to find a comfortable spot.

"You're right, sweetheart. He *is* honest in what he tells us. Still, I hoped we would have ended this by now."

We slid down under the covers for a long, well-deserved nap.

Early in the afternoon, I awoke well rested and as good as new. Well, *almost.* My leg reminded me otherwise every time my foot made contact with the floor. Layne begged to carry or transport me downstairs, but I figured a little walking would be good for me and help me stretch out my sore muscles.

"Good afternoon, everybody."

As set as I had been on the idea to walk from the bedroom down to the kitchen on my own, I had to admit I overestimated the distance and had to accept Layne's assistance from halfway down the stairs to my chair. Sitting down was never so welcomed.

Another strategy session with the entire group of panther hunters was getting underway.

"How you doing, gal? You didn't get any sleep last night, did you?" Daddy was concerned for me even though he was recovering from some cracked ribs himself after our encounter with Del in the pasture yesterday.

"I hope my tossing and turning didn't keep you all awake."

"He only heard you moving around because he insisted on walking the house from one end to the other every hour or so last night to keep an eye on the yard from every window in the house." Mama smiled and patted his arm as she passed the roast beef and bread.

"So, nobody's gettin' any sleep and we're no closer to resolving this than we were yesterday." Layne slapped a slice of beef between two pieces of bread and took an absent-minded bite.

I inhaled a deep breath and addressed the situation with my two cents worth. "Layne, since I didn't sleep very much last night, it gave me time to think. I had an idea and wanted you all to hear it." I anticipated the forthcoming objections to my latest idea but forged ahead anyway.

"Oh no. Lynzi, I don't think I'm gonna like where you're headed with this." Layne tossed his half-eaten sandwich onto his plate and shook his head.

"Now, Layne, listen first, and then we can all discuss this as adults." I placed my hand on his arm to calm him and buy myself a couple of minutes to propose my plan.

His head continued its side-to-side motion as if his mind was made up and his answer was a firm *no*.

"We all know Del has threatened to kill me. I say we give him his opportunity." I was cut short by some huffing and puffing from the man seated next to me but ignored it for the time being.

"You can't fight Del, Lynzi. His kind of mean only gets crazier when he's in cat form. He *will* kill you if he's given half a chance," Layne protested.

"Will you hush up and hear me out, please? We'll put some new calves in the barn. Lake and the boys can position themselves in the hayloft, Tom and his folks, too, without Del ever suspecting they're anywhere around. I'll walk out the back door and into the barn to check on the calves *alone* and if he's watching, he'll follow. Only *you* will be right by my side every step of the way. I'll be safe from every angle. When he follows me in, we close the doors tight, and we have him trapped. That's it. Tom can hold trial right then and there and this whole nightmare will all be over and done with." I glanced around the table to pick up on any signs of opposition. Nothing negative appeared on a single face in the room. I turned to the person most likely to give multiple objections. He remained still. At least his head had stopped shaking, which meant he was thinking about the *possibility* of this plan working. The silence was deafening and seemed to stretch on for, forever.

Lake spoke first. "Layne, I understand you wanting—needing to protect Lynzi and keep her safe. Me and the boys? We would die before we put her into *any* kind of danger. She is our sister. But you already know what's on our minds and you know we think it's a safe, workable plan." Lake took a breath but kept his focus on Layne, the person most likely to object.

"Lynzi and I could spend some time picking out new calves to replace the ones Del killed yesterday and put them in the barn here. You would be right by her side. If he's watching, and we're sure he will be, he'll see and hear everything. We can go our separate ways and later she, with you at her side can go out to the barn to check on them. We'll already be in and around the barn. Once he's in, we close the doors, and Tom gets his chance to deal with Del the way he sees fit. Everyone gets what they want, except in Del's case, he gets what he so rightly deserves."

Lake paused and turned to Tom. "As long as it's done in a way where he will *never* hurt another living soul again."

Tom nodded a resolute affirmation that the two were on the same level of thinking. Del's reign of terror would come to an end, once and for all, and very soon.

Lake turned back to Layne to get his answer. "I know you don't like it, but, Layne, it's solid."

It meant so much to me that Lake backed me on this. I'd never side with anyone against Layne but as Lake had said, this plan was a surefire way to end this nightmare. I turned to Layne who was still studying the crusts left from his sandwich.

After a somewhat lengthy pause, he turned to me and directed his gaze deep into my eyes. "I'll go along with the plan, but *not* today. I want you to take it easy and let your leg heal for another day. At least." Layne slid his fingers through my hair and cupped the side of my head. "I could never live with myself if I lost you. I *have* to be careful," he whispered as we gazed into each other's eyes.

"You're *not* going to lose me, Layne. I have you and the best guard teams in the world, both worlds, to keep me safe. We're gonna get this done." I caught a glimpse of Boone walking into the living room, deep in thought. "If Del thought killing those calves yesterday was pay back, he ain't seen nothing yet. Now, finish your lunch, I'll be back in a minute." I nodded toward the newest member of our family as I eased from my seat and limped after him into the living room.

I made my way to the opposite end of the couch and lowered myself with as much grace as my injuries would allow. Boone gently lifted my feet and inched them around to the seat high enough to slide a pillow underneath and elevate my aching leg. "Thanks. I thought you might want to talk. Are you okay with everything we have planned? I should have consulted you first. I'm sorry, but when I get an idea it sorta pops out before I stop to think." I shrugged my shoulders and allowed him time to answer. I couldn't imagine him having second thoughts, but I regretted not including him beforehand and wanted to get his input now.

"Oh, no, ma'am, Ms. Lynzi. I will never forgive Del for what he did to my mama. I want to get this over with as quick as we can. I am real worried about Jesse though. I owe it to Mama's memory to try to help him." He hung his head, obviously still blaming himself for not saving his mama, and without a word of concern for what he had suffered at the hands of his own father.

I reached over and took his hand in mine. "Do you want to be there when we pull the plan together?"

"Oh yes, ma'am, I want to see Del get what's coming to him. It won't bring Mama back but at least I'll know he paid for what he did."

11

The twenty-four-hour watch continued through the next day and night until Layne was halfway convinced I was healed and back to my old self. After breakfast, Lake and I, with Layne close by my side, spent an hour or so observing the herd behind the barn at our place.

"I like the young bull over by the fence. He already has a champion's stance. I can't say any one of the little heifers or steers is any better than the other. Y'all did such a good job picking out this herd to get me started in the beef cattle business. Now, with all the new calves this spring, the count has increased even with the losses. The Miller children will be pleased as punch with these calves and this time they should be safer in the Brady barn." I wanted each of the three children to have his own calf to raise and enter in the show at the county fair in the fall, and a healthy young bull and two heifers from our prize stock to start their own modest herd. I was so blessed to have everything I ever wanted out of life and now I could share a tiny bit of happiness with some children I took an immediate liking to after I got established here.

I was learning more every day about the business but most of this chatter between Lake and me today was meant to fuel the fire of Del's revenge. We hoped he was listening, prayed he would take the bait, and come after the calves again to get to me.

"I hope we've seen the last of Del and this nightmare is over. Open the gate and we'll move the new calves into the holding pen," Lake said. This would make it easy to load them onto the trailer to take to the Brady's barn for safe keeping in case we were wrong.

"You two should be actors," Layne whispered into my ear sounding his approval of the dialogue between Lake and myself. "I haven't seen any movement but I'm certain he's here, somewhere. The stench is unmistakable."

"I sure hope you're right." I chose my words to fit both Layne and Lake's last comments. I didn't want to alert Del that something other than what he could see with his own eyes was going on.

I had kept a close eye on the tree line at the edge of the pasture myself in case Del decided to show up again. I didn't see any movement, but I would bet my bottom dollar he was lurking, somewhere close by.

The trailer was ready to load the calves for transport to the Brady barn. This was my way of telling Del these calves were special, and I didn't want them killed like the last ones I had left here.

We took the short drive to the Brady's and secured the calves in the holding pens outside the barn before we made our way into the house. I planned to make one last trip to the barn after supper to secure them for the night. If our plan worked, Del would be there, and we could end this.

"I smelled cat coming from every direction, but I couldn't tell if it was Del or Tom and some of his folks. Then, there was that *unique* scent of a drunk. He was somewhere, I just couldn't pinpoint where," Layne said as he poured sweet tea into the glasses I had filled with ice cubes.

"I never caught sight of any movement either. Del doesn't strike me as being the sharpest knife in the drawer. How is he able to keep hidden so well?" Lake was as bewildered as the rest of us.

After lunch, Mr. Brady walked to the barn with us to inspect the lot and give his opinion on my selections.

"You picked a fine bunch to start those kids off with Lynzi gal. If we don't interest the children of today in farming and livestock production, the country is headed for a deeper downfall. We need more products made in the USA. That means more jobs for our people and more pride in this great country of ours." Daddy was a true patriot. He had spent years in the army himself protecting our country and the freedom we all love. Another reason he was included on my hero list.

We spent the rest of the afternoon cleaning stalls and bringing in fresh hay, making ourselves as visible as we could while completing the chores in and around the barn. The last chore was to secure the calves in the stalls inside the barn. We headed back into the house for supper and one last meeting to make sure everyone had memorized the assigned positions for the night.

Chef Woods was grill master for tonight's supper and had cooked up a pile of thick, juicy burgers while Mama deep fried a variety of fresh veggies and potatoes as well as some dill pickle slices. Boone joined in the family supper preparations by mixing a fruity, marshmallow fluff desert to spoon over fresh baked pound cake.

He grew more comfortable each day as a regular family member and loved helping in the kitchen. Family life agreed with him, and I was proud to be a part of the family he now called his own.

The last of the burgers disappeared along with the veggies and fries. Mama sliced the cake and Boone spooned his pink, fluffy dessert confectionary over the top of each slice as it was passed around the table.

By the time the dessert plates were cleaned, the sun had begun to set and signaled show time. The guards transported Boone into the barn to find a suitable, secluded spot for him until Del could be trapped inside, *if,* we were lucky enough to have our plan work.

I made my way out to the barn with my invisible shadow close by my side. The crickets chirped and the frogs croaked a lovely spring song. The first stars of the evening twinkled an invitation to sit and gaze skyward, snuggled with someone you love, *but* we had a job to do. I pushed forward to the barn door, swung it open, and flipped on the lights. "Hey, moo-moos, y'all ready for a bedtime snack?" I checked the water buckets and made sure there was plenty to drink before I grabbed a pitchfork, gathered several sections of hay, and moved toward the stalls to fill the racks for the calves.

The rusty hinge on the barn door creaked a warning that someone was entering. "Lake, did you decide to join me?" I turned with a big smile as if I were expecting to see Lake but had already learned from a whisper at my side that Del was sneaking through the door. My smile faded.

A scowl covered my face at the sight of that monster. "What do you want? Have you come back to kill these poor calves, too?" I poised with my pitchfork as I had on our last meeting here in the barn with the most disgusted expression I could muster, although it didn't take much effort. My loathing of Del was quite genuine.

"Maybe I will have me a snack after I settle some unfinished business with you, missy." He fumbled with his belt buckle as he grinned with blood-stained teeth. I wondered whose stock had been sacrificed for his supper in the last hour or so.

I realized Layne had stepped forward ready to deal with Del if he came any closer to me, but I wasn't sure why Lake and the boys had not closed the barn doors to get this showdown underway.

The picture became crystal-clear as soon as Del spoke again. "Jesse! Come on in here, boy. You need to see this." He ripped the belt from the loops at his waist, grasped the buckle, wrapped the strap around his hand a couple of times, and held it high above his head.

A young man about Boone's age, with a hefty chunk of fresh beef in one hand stepped through the barn door. He had facial features and a build like Boone but was the spitting image of Del in the personal hygiene department. Both had stringy, greasy hair, dirty clothes, and teeth that had never been introduced to a toothbrush. He ripped off a mouthful of beef, tossed the remainder of the chunk into the corner of the barn, and wiped his hands on his pants legs. Blood dripped from his chin as he chewed.

"You shouldn't oughta waste prime beef like that, boy," Del said with a sneer.

"Plenty more where that came from. Free for the takin', too." Jesse's smirk mimicked Del's. Birds of a feather. He was nothing like his brother. How in the world Boone ever turned out to be so kind and well-mannered was a mystery to me.

"You are both despicable. I find the mere sight of you repulsive."

"I done heard all your uppity mouth I'm gonna take, Miss High and Mighty. Jesse, go around that side, get behind her, and take that fork away from her. I'm gonna teach her a lesson she won't never forget." He held the belt as if he were going to use it on me the way he had on Boone and his mama. Right. Like that was *ever* going to happen.

I held fast to my weapon as I kept an eye on each of the werepanthers in front of me, aiming it at each one of them in turn as a warning. They moved in my direction but since Layne stood close to my back with his hand splayed across my stomach, ready to transport me out of harm's way, I'd never actually need to use it.

Before anyone could take another breath Boone leapt over the stall gate. He placed himself square in front of me, arms outstretched forming a barrier to protect me. Layne didn't move. I didn't need to read his mind. His body language spoke to me loud and clear. He remained still, realizing Boone *needed* to take care of this on his own. He had as much backup as necessary, but he needed to speak his piece.

"You're not going to lay a hand on her, Del! You have used that belt of yours on a woman for the last time! I'm not about to let that happen *ever* again," Boone stated, his voice strong and determined.

He stood in a protective stance, solid and confident as he turned to address his brother. "Jesse, there's no hope for him. He'll end up gettin' you killed if you stay with him. Tom said both of us can come back and be part of the clan again. All you have to do is step over here with me, we'll let Tom handle him, the panther way."

Del huffed out a sarcastic breath. "Tom's not here, now is he, boy? So, why don't you just get out of my way and let me take care of this damn witch? Then, I'm gonna deal with you for runnin' off again," he spouted off.

I could hear Layne's breathing become ragged and harder to control. His grip on me tightened slightly. He wanted to take matters into his own hands. I placed my hand over his on my stomach, locked our fingers together to ensure our heart-to-heart connection, and communicated the need to let Boone handle this.

"Think again, Del." Tom's voice rang out from the open doorway. He was backed by several dark-haired, muscular young men I took to be some of Tom's panthers. The Bradys had explained there was a panther council led by Tom who kept panther law and made decisions about the clan. I was certain the council had accompanied Tom to the barn tonight.

As they stepped inside, Del and Jesse gasped in utter surprise. Tom and his group formed a solid wall of muscle between the two of them and the only way out of the barn. Lake and his team secured the heavy wooden doors and stood aside until their help was requested.

Boone relaxed his shoulders a bit. "See, Jesse. We don't have to be afraid of Del anymore. He's gonna get what's comin' to him for all he did to Mama and to us all our lives. We never have to take those pills again. We can have lives of our own, Jesse. We can be happy." Boone sounded desperate to convince his brother that life without Del meant they would be free. Free of the domination they'd experienced. They had been prisoners all their lives. He paused to allow Jesse time to absorb the idea of freedom from Del's grasp and to join him.

Instead, Jesse held his stomach with one hand and doubled over laughing. He slapped his knee and pointed at Boone. "Pop always said you were a goody two shoes. He stopped giving me pills twelve or fifteen years ago when he was sure who he could trust. We kept you dosed up to keep you in line, you loser."

"But, Jesse, living his way is wrong. We can do better. We can work hard and make something of ourselves. Maybe have a place of our own one of these days."

Poor, sweet, Boone. His pleading fell on deaf ears. Jesse had been brainwashed by Del and didn't realize he was living a bad life.

Jesse boasted, "Why work when we can take anything we want, right Pop?"

Del grinned as if he were proud to have his son admit to being a thief and a lowlife. "That's right boy, we don't have nothin' tying us down. Come on now, forget about this traitor, and let's get out of here. I need a drink." He swung a cupped hand through the air, motioning for Jesse to follow him, but came up against a panther barrier.

"What you fail to realize Del is that you must pay for all you've done. You abused these boys all their lives, their mama, too, until you killed her. Now, you've led the slaughter of the livestock in the area and caused a hardship on everyone in this barn not to mention bodily harm on Mr. Brady and Lynzi. It's time you answered for all your crimes." Tom stood tall and waited for Del to admit he had caused all this pain and suffering to his family, the clan, and to the people he had robbed.

"I ain't done nothin' and you can't prove it. Ellen. Sh-she ain't dead. She, she run off. Now, you let me outta here, Tom Monroe. I ain't done nothin' I tell ya." Wild-eyed, his head jerked in every direction searching for an ally or maybe an escape route. But there were none. No one to defend him and no way out of the barn.

"You said them spells your woman put around us would kill our scent." Jesse's eyes flashed with wildness. "You said nobody would know it was us and we'd get clean away with it!" He searched the faces of everyone in the barn until he stopped on Boone's. "You told them!" He screeched and pointed a finger still stained and wet with blood from the fresh beef. "You turned on us! You set this trap!" He screamed and lunged toward Boone.

Layne tightened his grip on me, and we reappeared in the hayloft above the forthcoming fracas. He remained invisible but continued to hold me in his protective embrace. My heart lunged into my throat. I worried for Boone's safety. "Boone," I whispered. I didn't want to distract him by calling out his name and causing him to be hurt.

Del screamed a mad panther cry as he, too, scrambled toward Boone. Two of Tom's panthers each grabbed an arm and held fast to prevent any further movement on his part. Boone appeared frozen to the floor, unable to move. His brother's rejection had traumatized the poor boy, as I feared it would.

Before he made contact, Tom dove forward and slammed into Jesse with enough force to send them both tumbling down. They rolled several times. Locked in death grips, they both growled as each tore at the others flesh.

My heart cried out for Boone who stood and watched as the two engaged in battle. Tom, the bulkier, more powerful of the two, paused several times to give the boy a chance to give himself up. "Back off, Jesse, and let's talk about this like grown men. I know you were forced into this, but I'll give you a chance to prove yourself if you'll take it."

Jesse refused to stop. He would shake it off, utter a vicious growl, and storm forward for another round.

In the intensity of the fight, the animalistic survival instinct took over and the pair shifted into panther form right before my eyes. Amazing and frightening to see and hear human bones crack and reconstruct into animal shape. Muscles ripped and reformed. Raven fur appeared and covered their bodies.

I shuddered at the sight and sounds of the transformation and covered my mouth with my hand to suppress my gasp. Layne held firm to me as they continued the change from human to cat form. Two full-grown black panthers now circled each other on the barn floor below us and growled their warnings to each other. As long as they moved at a slow pace, I could distinguish between the two but as soon as they tied up again, they were more like one giant fur ball rolling on the floor, screaming, and growling.

Even in animal form, the panther leader made several failed attempts to persuade Jesse to stand down. A powerful paw swung through the air, smacking Jesse on the shoulder. The force slammed his body to the floor, rolling him several feet away. Tom paused and waited for the boy to surrender but Jesse insisted on getting up and going after his opponent again and again until his madness peaked. Foam dripped from the sides of Jesse's mouth. He had gone mad.

Tom ended the battle with a final bite locked onto Jesse's throat. The younger panther shrieked in pain as he thrashed about on the floor, the life draining from his torn and mangled neck. Finally, his body stilled, and he lay limp.

Tom stood panting over the lifeless body for a moment to catch his breath before slinking off behind the wall of panther guards. When he reappeared, he was in human form, and completely dressed again. I noticed each of his guards had a backpack strapped on and figured extra clothing or provisions were carried in this manner when they expected changing forms would be in order.

No one spoke. The barn became quiet again.

12

Layne kept a firm grip around my waist for our return trip to Boone's side. He stood in silence and disbelief, his eyes glued to his brother's dead body, crumpled on the barn floor.

"You did this, witch! My boy is dead and it's all your fault!" Del screeched his accusations. The veins in his neck and forehead bulged to a throbbing blue-purple color. Spittle flew from his mouth and dripped down his chin. His red, bloodshot eyes protruded so that they threatened to pop from their sockets.

He was even more convinced I was some kind of witch now. With Layne still hidden from sight, it appeared I had moved from the ground floor of the barn up to the hayloft and back under some of my own magical power.

His enraged state may have been mistaken for some kind of emotion over the death of his son but from where I stood, he was trying to find someone, anyone, to blame for the path he had chosen in creating his pathetic life.

"Tom, Tom, she killed them cows and set me and Jesse up to take the fall! You gotta believe me! You and me Tom, we're panther brothers, we gotta stick together." He pointed in my direction as he stuttered and begged for his freedom.

"Boone has told us the whole story Del. As panther leader, I declare you guilty, and by panther law, you must pay for all your crimes. And for the record, let's get one thing straight, you and I are *not* brothers, and we are *nothing* alike." Tom had made his decision. The evidence was overwhelming.

"Boone's a lie. He's the sorriest excuse for a son there ever was. Never helped support his family. Always running off. He's lying, I tell ya! His mama's alive! She just run off." Del snarled, gritting out the words, then spat on the floor.

I had heard quite enough out of him. I peeled Layne's hand from my stomach, marched right up to Del, looked him square in the eyes, and said, "Boone is a wonderful young man. He's already a thousand times the man you are. He *will* realize all his dreams and become whatever he decides to be. You don't deserve to breathe the same air as him."

Outraged at the thought of that sweet boy and all he had suffered; I drew back and slapped Del's sorry face with all the force I could muster. My hand stung like fire from the impact with the stubble on his unshaven jowl. Shock waves of pain rang through the muscles in my right arm, and I shook with rage of my own, but it was only a drop in the bucket of what he deserved. I could read his expression that any type of retribution delivered by a female was the utmost humiliation for him. Good.

The veins in his neck bulged and threatened to burst. He spit a steady stream of profanity in my direction as he struggled for his freedom from the two holding him, but Tom's men held tight to their prisoner. I stood steady and tall, raised my chin with a tightened jaw, and held my position to emphasize my point. I wasn't afraid of him. His words couldn't hurt me. Besides, Lake and his team as well as Layne had moved closer to support my need to say my piece and to ensure my safety while doing so.

"Get him out of here. Take him to the clearing by the rock formation and hold him there. I'll be along. Two of you take this body to the cemetery and get a space ready. We owe it to Ellen to give her son a proper burial." Tom watched as Del was dragged, kicking and screaming, out of the barn and to the location where he would pay for his crimes against the panthers and their way of life, as well as their neighbors.

Jesse's body was wrapped in a tarp and carried out to his final resting place in the panther cemetery on Tom's land.

"I want to thank all of you for letting me take care of this in our way. I'll make sure we clean up all the mess that was made tonight." He waved a hand over the bloody spot where Jesse had died and toward the lump of beef that had been discarded in the corner of the barn earlier. There had to be a dead cow or cows somewhere near judging by the five-pound chunk of beef. Tom's clean up would take the better part of the night.

Our duty at this moment was to the frightened boy standing in shock behind me. "Layne, we need to get Boone inside the house. He's been through enough for one evening." I turned to find him in the exact spot where he had come to my rescue earlier. I placed my hand on his cheek and eased his head around to face me. We made eye contact, and I searched for any sign he could hear my voice. I was sure we connected when a slight whimper escaped his lips and tears filled his eyes. "Boone. We need to go inside now." I waited to make sure he understood and was willing to go along with us.

He gave a slight nod confirming his comprehension before he spoke. "I can't believe Jesse's dead, too." He returned his stare to the spot where his brother's body had been.

I offered him my hand. When he accepted, we made our way out of the barn and toward the house. In the kitchen, Aunt Pet had a steamy cup of tea ready for Boone. Her healing tea was like a fix-all remedy. It was good for what ailed you and healed all sorts of wounds. In Boone's case, it would help with the hole in his heart, help relax and calm him so he could begin to deal with all that was said and done tonight. He'd had such high hopes for a life with his brother and now, even though he would always have people near who cared deeply for him, he was alone.

Aunt Pet set the cup in front of him as he settled at the table. She stroked his hair in a soothing manner, "Time and tea will help to heal your wounds. Your magic has much potential. Your heart will heal stronger than before, young Boone."

Did I hear correctly? My mouth dropped open slightly as I ran possibilities over in my mind. "Magic? What do you mean, Aunt Pet? I wasn't aware that werefolk had any magical abilities?" My knowledge of magical and mystical affairs was far from complete. I had much more to learn and sensed a new lesson was right around the corner.

"We weren't sure until now, sweetheart, but even though Boone has full panther abilities, he's only part panther. His mama was half witch, remember? Aunt Pet read his other side when she touched him and sensed he has some magical abilities as well. To what extent will be seen in time."

I recalled Layne's dream lesson from the other day. Many beings exist with different abilities and there was good and bad in all. I was sure Boone, like Aunt Pet and the others in our Fae family, would follow his heart and use his magic, whatever that might be, for only good.

"I don't know if I want any magic. I don't even know if I want to be a panther anymore. My whole family is dead. It didn't help any of them. None of our abilities helped any of them." Boone stared into his tea. The same dazed expression had covered his face since Jesse revealed the truth about his relationship with Del, that he had been favored over Boone and even helped manipulate him over the years by keeping him drugged.

"The entire being must desire to be whole. The heart is the core of the being. If the mind does not abide by what the heart desires, there is not a proper balance. You have that balance, young Boone." Aunt Pet poured more tea into his cup. "Drink your tea. All will be clearer after you sleep."

Boone lifted the cup to his lips and drew in a long sip of the warm, soothing tea. "Are you saying my mama *didn't* have a good heart?" Even more confusion clouded a shocking situation.

"I think she's saying there was some sort of, disconnect, between your mama's good heart and her mind." I turned to Aunt Pet and raised my hands to question any correction or addition needed to my assumption of her statement.

"Not a good connection. Yes. Her heart led her to help but her mind followed the wrong paths." Aunt Pet tried again to explain the link between a good heart and the actions backing it up.

"And what about Jesse and Del?" Boone needed answers and we needed to help him understand. "I guess it doesn't take a genius to figure out Del didn't *have* a heart or a good mind but, *Jesse?* I thought Jesse and me were alike." He propped his elbow on the table and rested his cheek on his fist. As he stared into his cup, a tear trickled down his cheek.

My heart was breaking. I wanted to do or say something to make his hurt go away. But as Aunt Pet said, only time would ease his pain. I had another idea. "Layne, would you help me with something in the living room, please?" I headed for the other room with a big idea rolling around in my head and I needed to run it by my expert.

I took his hands in mine and stood on my tiptoes to whisper my thoughts. "Layne, Boone will be relaxed enough to sleep soon according to Aunt Pet. Do you think you could give him a dream to brighten his outlook on the future? Something to give him hope? I can't stand to see him hurting like this. It's breaking my heart."

He smiled and shook his head. "Girl, you have more love in that heart of yours than anyone will ever know." He wrapped me tight in his arms. "That's one of the best ideas I've heard today. As soon as he's asleep, I'll step in and give him a dream to dream. Anything special you'd like me to suggest to him?"

"Well, we know from what he told Jesse, he wants to have a place of his own someday. And we know that he's lost his family. Those are two of his dreams for the future, home and family. If he could see what life can be like sharing it with someone he loves, maybe it would plant a seed. What do you think?" I wanted to do something to help that poor boy have a flicker of hope for the future. Show him there is life beyond the horrors he suffered all his life and the ones he had witnessed in the barn tonight, not that I could do anything except come up with the idea. Layne would have to do all the work.

"Let's go see if the tea has calmed him down enough to sleep." Layne smiled and gave me a squeeze.

I was excited to be a part of the plan to show Boone how happy life can be. After all, I was living, breathing proof that life can go from ordinary to extraordinary in the blink of an eye.

I took a step toward the kitchen only to be stopped by a gentle tug on my hand. As I turned back, Layne's hands framed my face. He gazed deep into my eyes. "If I can show him a future with a smidgen of the happiness in my heart right now, he'll be just fine." Our lips brushed together with a feather-light touch. We inhaled the scent that was ours alone. One that fueled the fire of our passion for each other. I stepped closer and locked my arms around his waist as he enveloped me. "I pray we can help him through this so he can find the happiness we have." I snuggled into his embrace and gave thanks for my blessing of happiness.

"It is time for young Boone to sleep now." Aunt Pet whispered breaking the silence around us and drawing our attention from the flames dancing inside us.

"I'll go with him upstairs and make sure he gets settled into bed. And if you're about ready to turn in sweetheart, I'll meet you in our room." Layne kissed my hand and headed for the kitchen.

"Do you think he'll be all right, Aunt Pet?" We watched as Layne followed Boone upstairs.

"Yes, yes, my little one. He is strong. Time will fade the bad memories, and he will grow even more resilient. You will see." She squeezed my hand as I breathed a sigh of relief. Aunt

Pet only spoke of what she was certain would come to be. That much I was sure of.

"Thank you for all your help, Aunt Pet. I'm glad we're going to have a happy ending to Boone's story. Are you going back to the ranch tonight?"

"No, little one, I am off to Texas to meet with Cloi about the plans for our big event," she replied with a twinkle in her eyes.

"Thank you again for all your hard work on the wedding. I'm so excited. It's hard to believe Layne and I are finally going to be married." Now that this disaster was behind us, for the most part, I could allow myself to become excited about our wedding again.

"It will be so, and then, your family will grow." There was that twinkle again.

"Yes, ma'am, it will. And I'm going to need your advice and help every step of the way."

"You shall have it, my little one, and now I must be on my way."

I smiled as I bent to kiss her cheek. "Good night." She shimmered and left my sight.

Layne eased the door to Boone's room closed as I topped the stairs. He winked and nodded toward our bedroom. Good. The dream planting was a success. Boone would see now what the future could offer if he moved on with his mind *and* heart set on a good life.

The lock clicked on our door as my happy future led me to the bathroom and began to undress me with the slightest movement of his finger. A playful smile spread across his face as he pointed to my shirt and the floor indicating what article of clothing he wanted removed and where he wanted it to fall. Magically, my shirt removed itself and dropped to the right, jeans to the left. My bra and panties followed but he paused at that point leaving the two of us in much different degrees of dress. Though I stood before him naked as the day I came into the world, his focus was on my eyes. The sly smile subsided as he studied me. His expression accentuated an array of emotions. Desire. Passion. Fear.

I understood each one since they also gripped my heart with a fierce ache. My own desire and passion burned inside for a life with Layne, but the fear that we would be separated again lingered.

My craving for his touch increased to a glaring urge. I needed to have his skin on my skin, to absorb the warmth radiating from his body, mingled with my own in exchange. He inhaled a deep cleansing breath.

Now, I needed to deal with the barrier of his jeans and shirt between us. "The playing field is more than a bit uneven from where I stand," I whispered to draw his attention. That mischievous curl of his lips returned as he nodded and raised a finger toward his shirt. I nodded in agreement with his suggestion. The shirt unbuttoned itself one button at a time in a gradual, deliberate motion, and slid from his arms only to return hastily, bringing a gasp of surprise from me. I had expected it to flutter to the floor alongside mine but now it was buttoned as before.

My astonished expression was exactly the reaction he was going for by the low chuckle and the *gotcha* grin he now sported. "Not fair. Show me what you got, cowboy." I propped my hands on my hips in protest and produced another teasing chuckle from the performer on stage in our bathroom.

The shirt eased its way down his arms again and came to rest at his waist. He stood motionless as the button of his jeans slipped free, and the zipper inched its way down to allow his shirt the freedom to flutter to the floor. This time my eyes roamed over the sight before me. The jeans slipped down a few inches and back up in another teasing manner before they disappeared, leaving him in his black silk boxers.

Only in my wildest dreams did I ever imagine I would be audience to a magical strip show performed for my eyes alone. I thought I'd try my hand at maneuvering clothing. I pointed to his boxers and then to the floor. Of course, nothing happened. Human fingers aren't loaded with magic, but assistance was on the way.

Layne repeated my gestures, pointing to his boxers, then to the floor, and grinned when I nodded. They slowly drifted to the floor. Now we're getting somewhere. I tried my magic finger once again and wiggled it as I stepped into the shower beckoning him to follow. What do you know? It worked.

Still warm from the shower we sank into bed, entwined ourselves into a single embrace, and settled in for a restful night, each holding our future tight. Even with the turmoil we had been through the past few days, the simple act of being wrapped in Layne's arms assured me all was right with the world.

We slept in a peaceful slumber until bloodcurdling panther screams rocked the still of the night.

What now?

13

My heart pounded in my chest from being awakened from a sound sleep by terrifying animalistic screams outside our room. I scrambled out of bed and toward the source of the disturbance, with Layne not far behind. Boone's room. We found him curled into a ball, face down in his pillow. He grasped fists full of hair tight in both hands and rocked on his knees.

"No! No! Stop!" he cried over and over, rolling back and forth on the bed.

"Lynzi, go back in the bedroom and lock the door behind you. He could shift any second without realizing. He's dangerous right now." Layne always put my safety first, but Boone would never harm me.

"It's still Boone. He's not going to hurt me." I took another step toward the bed. "Boone. Boone wake up, everything's okay." I reached out and touched his shoulder. "Boone. It's Lynzi. Wake up now. No one's going to hurt you. You're with friends. You're safe." I rubbed his shoulder and gave him a slight shake to bring him out of this nightmare that was apparently consuming him.

After a few seconds, he stilled. His sobs subsided. He lay quiet for a moment before he came to his knees, raising his head. His eyes remained closed. He stretched his neck and leaned his head back to face the ceiling. His mouth opened and another scream pierced the silence.

"Lynzi!" Layne yanked me behind him in a split second and directed his attention toward Boone. "Boone. Listen to my voice. Wake up now. Wake up. You're safe. This is only a dream." Layne's voice was smooth and calm. It worked. Boone relaxed. His rigid body unwound and calmed. He opened his eyes and searched the room to reacquaint himself with his surroundings. Finally, he settled his gaze on his two bewildered visitors.

"Layne, Ms. Lynzi. What are you‑‑?" He paused. His eyes roamed the room again. He eased his body around, sat on the edge of the bed, and ran his hand through his hair.

"Boone, what happened?" I stepped around Layne and stood at his side wondering how one of Layne's pleasant dreams could produce such a fierce reaction.

"It was Del. He was beatin' Mama and me, and you too, Ms. Lynzi. I tried, but I couldn't stop him. He just kept on and on, laughing and laughing." Boone shook his head with an expression of confusion and fear.

I turned to Layne for an answer to the one question running through my mind and I was sure it was a mystery to him as well. I extended both hands asking silently. How did this happen? Layne had given him a happy dream to dream, and Del had somehow invaded it from his grave. Happy dreams *always* worked for me. Where had this nightmare starring that monster come from?

The Bradys remained cautiously quiet at the door. Mrs. Brady had the best solution of the moment. "Why don't we all meet in the kitchen? I'll go get the coffee started."

"Thanks, Mama. We'll get dressed and be right down." I eased passed Layne to the door and turned to Boone. "It was just a dream, Boone. He's gone for good now and we're both safe." He nodded; his gaze still focused on the floor. The pain from the monster that tormented his dreams hung like a dark, threatening cloud around him. I shared a confused glance with Layne as I went to get dressed.

Layne closed our bedroom door with a befuddled expression as I stepped from the bathroom pulling my hair into a ponytail. "Darlin', I don't know what went wrong. Nothing like this ever happened when I gave *you* a dream. Maybe it was too soon after watching his brother die or, I-I don't have a clue." He raised his hands in question, wondering the same as me. What was going in Boone's subconscious just waiting to come out?

"Layne, honey. Stop blaming yourself. We need more information. Why don't you have Aunt Pet meet us for breakfast? Maybe she has some knowledge of what might have happened. We can talk and sort this all out." I took his hands in mine and kissed each one as I waited for him to agree with my suggestion. "Get dressed so we can hear *all* the details of the dream straight from Boone. Then maybe we'll better understand."

Layne nodded and closed his eyes. It was obvious he was plenty bothered that the dream he had given Boone to help brighten his future hadn't worked out as we had planned. I eased my way into his arms and snuggled close, holding him to reassure him we *would* figure out this latest mess.

"Aunt Pet's here," he said as he slipped on his jeans and shirt and followed me out into the hallway. Boone's door was open enough to see him. He still sat on the side of the bed and stared at the floor between his feet. "Hey, we're going downstairs. You take your time and come down when you're ready. Mama's got coffee started."

"Thanks, Layne. I sure am sorry for getting everybody up so early." Boone's eyes were red and tired as if he hadn't slept a minute.

I prayed we would find a solution to his inner torment so he could be at peace with himself and move on with his life and dreams.

At the table, Aunt Pet sat sipping coffee with the family. Layne hurried to her side and took his seat. "I'm so glad to see you. Did Mama and Daddy tell you what happened? Did Boone's sorrow over losing his brother override the dream I gave him? Did I confuse the matter and end up causing this?"

My poor Layne was worried he had added to Boone's misery and somehow *triggered* his nightmare. His heart was so good that it hurt him to think he had caused someone else pain.

"You worry too much, my darling. We will have all our answers as soon as young Boone is present." Aunt Pet brushed his cheek with the palm of her hand tiny hand to soothe his concern.

My need to comfort Layne *and* Boone was strong, but I wasn't sure how effective I could be. It certainly wouldn't keep me from trying my best though.

Boone shuffled across the floor in his sock feet and joined the family already assembled at the table. He settled into a chair and began an unnecessary apology as if he woke everyone before dawn on purpose. "I'm sorry, y'all. But it was *so* real. Like Del was alive. He was swingin' that belt and laughin' every single time it made contact. It was so loud. It popped and cracked and––" Boone shook his head trying to make sense of all this.

"Boone, did you have any other dreams last night?" Layne needed to learn if his dream had been overridden by Boone's nightmare.

"Yeah, I kept having one over and over, best dream I ever had." He closed his eyes briefly and smiled. Obviously, something pleasant happened at some point in his dreams. "I didn't want it to end but then Del came in and started beatin' everybody." Boone stopped as if the mention of Del's name interfered with his happy dream memories. His smile at the memory of his pleasant dream faded.

"This must be hard for you Boone, but could you start from the beginning and tell us exactly what you dreamed? Did Del show up in your good dream?" I thought we could better assess the situation if we had all the facts of the events in the order they happened.

"I didn't think I'd be able to sleep after everything that happened in the barn, but I drifted off as soon as my head hit the pillow and started dreaming. I had, a *family*." He paused and smiled as if he were replaying the scene in his mind. "I stood on the porch of a house, *my* house, and watched a little girl, *my* little girl, swinging in a wooden swing hanging from a big ol' oak tree in the backyard. A pretty, blond lady came out the back door and handed me a glass of tea. She was expecting another baby. *My* wife. *My* baby. We sat in rocking chairs and laughed and talked."

A short huff accompanied a proud smile. "The little girl on the swing sang songs. All her words floated in the air above her head. There were shapes like the notes in Ms. Sara's piano books. Only they were all pink and curly. They were the sweetest sounds I've ever heard. There was a barn and fenced pastures with cows and sheep. It was mine. *Ours*. I was happy. *We* were happy." He paused as if replaying the scenes again in his mind and smiled. His pleasant expression slowly faded as he continued.

"Then, these dark clouds came over and everything disappeared. My family, my house, my farm. Del just popped in slingin' that belt around. More dark clouds and black fog came rollin' in then cleared out and he'd be hittin' Mama. The clouds and fog would come back like curtains closing and opening and he was hittin' Ms. Lynzi. I tried to stop him, but he pushed me down and started hittin' me. I couldn't stop him. No matter how hard I fought, it didn't do any good. That's when you woke me up." He held his head in his hands and closed his eyes.

The poor boy must be exhausted. My heart ached to take his pain away.

"It is not Del. We all know he is gone. Someone else has entered young Boone's dream world and clouded his mind with images to cause distress and pain." Aunt Pet appeared confident in her assessment of the situation.

"Someone like--?" I prayed Aunt Pet could give us a name but then that would be too easy. Way too easy.

"It is magic. A spell was cast on young Boone as he slept. It altered his normal sleep, and the dream Layne gave him." She was unable to give us any clue as to the identity of the person casting the spell.

"Someone able to cast magical spells was in the house after we went to bed last night?" I gasped in horror at the thought of some stranger walking around the house while we all slept.

We could have been murdered in our sleep. I turned to Layne for any idea he had. He shook his head as a negative, no clue as to who had entered the house while we slept or what they may have done while in here. I had to ask, "What else did they do?"

Layne picked up on my concern or most likely had the same concerns. "Aunt Pet, we need the protection wards around this property as well as ours to protect Lynzi and my parents. We need to find this person and deal with them. But who would know or even care that Boone is staying here now? Del and Jesse are both dead." Questions to a puzzle we needed to assemble as soon as possible, before any of us lay down to sleep again.

What did the magical stranger who had roamed about our house and invaded Boone's dreams have in store for us tonight? We sat in silence, staring into our coffee mugs, hoping to find answers.

14

"Mena." Boone continued his coffee mug search as he spoke. "It's got to be Mena. She's the witch who left here with Del years ago. When Mama found him, he was with her. They had a big fight. Mena left but she was always close around. Always rubbed it in and let Mama know she was there. Her and Del would take off for days together then she'd drop him off at the house and drive away. But not before she let Mama know she was watching us, and she would have the last say. That must be it. She knows Del's dead and she's out to get even with *me* for it."

"Great. Just great. *Another* crazy person to deal with. But how?" I waited for our resident magical folks to give some direction. No suggestions or strategies were laid out to plan a workable solution. We all sat in silence.

Boone finished off his coffee and took his mug to the sink. "If y'all don't mind, I need to go for a run before daylight. It'll help clear my head. I sure am sorry for bringing more trouble on you good folks." He lowered his head in silence and started for the back door.

I stood to block his exit for a moment. "Boone, don't you go worrying about trouble. We'll figure this out. That's what family does. Oh, and did you forget something?" I pointed at his sock feet to remind him of his shoes or in this case, the lack of shoes.

He smiled and said, "I won't need them this time Ms. Lynzi, but thank you. For everything." He gave me a gentle pat on my arm.

The light bulb in my head flickered on. "Oh, I see. A different kind of run?" Layne had explained that the werepanther's inner animal needed to come out every now and again for some primal exercise. It was a balance thing between the animal and the human side.

His grin widened and he nodded. "Yes, ma'am."

"This is good. You go for your run, young Boone. And when you return with a clear mind, we will begin the work necessary to solve this problem." Aunt Pet spoke with the kind of confidence that filled me with encouragement. Our problem was as good as solved.

"Yes, Ma'am." Boone slipped out the back door into the pre-dawn morning.

"You have some ideas, Aunt Pet?" Layne poured more coffee for the five early risers still at the table while we waited for some direction.

"Yes, yes. Ideas. Now, I must go to the ranch for a brief time, but I shall return." The wheels were turning in that petite head of hers which meant a plan was forming. Mercy. Please let this one be quick and final.

"What about the protection wards? How soon can you place them around the properties?" Layne asked, eager to protect the humans so dear to him.

"I fear the protection wards would only reveal our presence to the witch causing additional problems, my darling. Other arrangements must be made." Aunt Pet delivered the news none of us wanted to hear but gave him a hug as she departed. "All will be well, my darling. You will see. You will see."

The four of us stared at each other for a bit, speechless. Aunt Pet had a plan. That much was for sure. I shuddered to think it involved leaving ourselves wide open to an attack again tonight. How comforting.

"Lynzi, I think you should go back to the ranch until this is settled. There'll be no protection on the house, and we don't even know what we're up against. Mama and Daddy, you should go, too. It'll be a vacation. Y'all haven't visited in a while. It'll be fun." Layne continued to try and convince us leaving was a good idea.

I turned my head in Mama's direction. As soon as our eyes met, we both snickered. "He's so funny sometimes," she managed to get out through the laughter.

"But he *is* cute Mama, you have to admit that." Our laughter continued.

"I am serious, you two. We don't know what this crazy witch has up her sleeve. We don't even know what she's capable of. I don't want you to be in the line of fire. Is it wrong for a man to want to protect his family?" Layne's frustration rang out loud and clear. And rightly so, but there was no way I was going to hide away and from her reaction, neither was Mama.

"Now, why don't we wait for Pet to come back and see what she has in mind before we make any plans?" Daddy's voice was one of reason in this case, although I couldn't see him being tucked away for safe keeping either. "If she's figured a quick fix for our latest mess and this can be tied up in one night, I think we can all come together and agree on the best way for everybody to stay safe."

Would I ever be educated enough in this, out of this world life to understand all the ins and outs of existence here? Lately, it seemed there was a different danger around every corner. Would *this* evil win?

15

The curtains on the door swayed as Boone opened it and leaned against the jamb to stretch his socks over his feet.

"Is that a genuine smile on your face?" The run appeared to have rejuvenated the werepanther. He huffed out a breath and wiped the sweat beads from his forehead.

"Yes, Ma'am. A run like that makes a new man out of me and I'm ready to take on the world." A newfound confidence radiated from him as he made his way to the table.

"Taking on the world sounds like a huge responsibility. I think you'd best have some breakfast first." I set a platter of hot biscuits on the table and turned back to the fridge for the butter, jellies, and fruit preserves.

With the Del situation behind us, and the cattle safe once again, Lake and the boys had returned to the ranch on the other side. They would resume their normal schedule of patrolling there and seeing to the daily guard duties while still making periodic visits here to tend the livestock on Lake's place and take care of business on this side.

Cubed steak, gravy, scrambled eggs with cheddar cheese, and biscuits for six was a faster fix in the mornings being about half as many mouths to feed. I poured another round of coffee as Aunt Pet appeared in her seat, hand basket in tow.

"Please tell us you've found everything we need to get rid us of this latest plague," Layne said as soon as Daddy finished

131

asking blessings on our breakfast and the new situation we now faced.

"Good morning to you also, my darling." She smiled as she fumbled inside her basket, brought out a small green glass bottle, and placed it on the table in front of her.

"Sorry, Aunt Pet. Good morning. How are you?" Layne leaned over, placed a sweet kiss on her cheek, and stroked her hair. He was sincere with his greeting, just a bit late, and slightly embarrassed he had to be prompted.

"An empty bottle? Shouldn't it be full of, *witch repellant*, Pet?" Daddy asked as he reached for another biscuit.

"Not empty for long. We must collect a few items for the bottle to activate the collection spell and wait for the witch to appear. The ingredients will draw the evil one inside. Once she is trapped, the bottle will be corked and tossed into a fire. It will explode and take the witch with it so she can no longer perform her evil magic." She appeared confident and quite pleased with herself. I hoped the plan would work. It sounded simple enough, maybe too simple. I took my bottom lip between my teeth and held my breath for the catch.

Layne pressed for the details. "Throwing a bottle into a fire and waiting for it to explode is easy. We're pretty sure the witch will be back to mess with Boone's dreams again tonight. I'm positive you can handle casting the spell." He paused and drew in a deep breath. "Now, for the items we need to *collect*. I have my doubts as to how easy *that* part is going to be."

"I never said easy, my darling. What we need is some wine, fresh rosemary sprigs, sharp pins and needles to capture the evil, and a personal item from the witch. Hair or trimmings from her nails will be sufficient."

And there it was. The catch.

"I have plenty of straight pins I use when I'm quilting, there's a healthy patch of rosemary in my herb garden, and several bottles of your rosebud wine in the pantry. Now heaven knows, I'd like to snatch that trouble-making witch bald for what she did last night, but I don't think she's going to knock on our door and introduce herself." Mama made the obvious point. "How in the world do we get some of her hair or, for heaven's sake, collect her nail trimmings?" The question we all needed answered.

"That part will be worked out by Boone and me after I get y'all settled safely on the other side at the ranch for a few days. The property there *is* protected by Aunt Pet's wards." Layne had put together another steak biscuit with a dollop of gravy tucked inside and took a big bite before he noticed all eyes focused on him. "What?" he asked in a muffled sound around the biscuit filling his mouth.

"Layne Brady don't talk with your mouth full. I taught you better manners than that. And I also taught you that I don't back down from a situation when my family is at risk. I'm staying right here and that's that." Mama had set back in her chair and propped her hands on her hips demonstrating her determination.

Layne swallowed and looked to his daddy for some support. Daddy returned an amused expression as he tried hard to keep from laughing. A quick glance toward Boone revealed a, *you're on your own since I don't have a clue how to handle this* expression.

Daddy chuckled as he spoke up to rescue his son. "Layne, the witch was here last night and didn't harm anyone else. Her target is Boone. That much is plain. I don't think we're in any danger from her at this point."

"Is it so wrong to want to keep my family safe? Wrong to protect you all and keep you from harm? I'm trying to do the right thing here." More than a hint of frustration accompanied his concern for our safety.

Bless his sweet, loving heart. He *was* only trying to protect us. I took his hand in mine. "Layne, baby, there's nothing at all wrong with you wanting to protect us, just as there's nothing wrong with us wanting to support and protect you. You are so sweet for caring. But why don't we see what we can accomplish today, and then decide where everyone goes for the night? Okay?" I wanted to be beside him every step of the way but if I could best ease his mind by being at the ranch, that was where I would be.

"The big question right now is, how do we get Mena's personal possession?" Boone made sure he swallowed his food and wiped his mouth before he posed his question. I'm sure he didn't want to get on Mama's bad side.

"Does anyone know where she lives? Finding her would be the first step to getting what we needed to fill our witch bottle." I was a list person, and first on the list in my mind would be locating Mena.

"She's got family living over on Sawmill Road. That's where Del stayed most of the time. I'm sure she's still there. I could take a run over and check it out." Boone was eager to end this. We all were.

"It might not be a good idea to let her see you, Boone." Layne seemed deep in thought. "Now, *I* could slip in without being seen, grab her hairbrush, and be back here before anybody could say jack rabbit."

"Right, and what if someone's in the room, and sees her hairbrush floating around on its own? They're witches, Layne. Do you know for sure they can't see you or detect your presence somehow? And besides, how would you know her brush from any of the others in the house? What happens if you get the wrong brush?" I wasn't about to allow him to run headlong into danger. I didn't *say* the word *allow* so he could hear, mind you. I made sure it was contained securely in my thoughts. "You would need a distraction. Now, if I stopped by to ask for say, directions––"

"Lynzi––" I kind of figured his voice would increase an octave or two on the last syllable of my name. I was right. "Don't even think about it."

"He's right, Ms. Lynzi. You can't go over there. All of them may be as crazy Mena is. No telling what they might do. Stands to reason if Del thought you were a witch he bad mouthed you to them and they all know who you are by now." Boone was becoming quite the protector himself. A good man. My heart smiled.

"I understand the need to rid yourselves of this witch as soon as possible but I must ask you to listen before you act. Young Boone has indicated there are multiple witches in the house. Witches are family, as we are, and will more than likely have planning sessions such as the one we are engaged in now. If the one interrupting young Boone's dreams disappears, we might unleash the wrath of the remaining witches." Aunt Pet had put the brakes on our avenue of thinking by unveiling this possibility.

Back to square one. Everyone stared into their breakfast plates as if answers were scrambled in with the eggs and our task was to unscramble them. That shouldn't be so hard. Yeah, right.

"Seems the first question we need answered is how many witches live in the house?" I had to step back and begin the thinking process all over.

"Sara darlin', when the preacher makes his rounds doing visitation, he keeps a log of the homes he visits and the family members living there, right?"

Wait a minute. Daddy just might be on to something.

"I believe so, Will. Why?"

"Well, he's been after me to go out with the visitation team and invite folks around the area to Sunday Services. I could go up to the church to schedule a night to make the rounds with him and get a look-see at the log. It might have the information we need if he's visited in that area before."

"We could also post an invisible guard at the house around the clock to watch the comings and goings of everyone there as soon as we have their names," Layne added to the safer plan to gather all the facts before we form a plan of action.

"Sounds like a more cautious plan but not one we can complete before bedtime. What's Boone supposed to do, stay awake until we find out where Mena is and who she has as her back up?" I couldn't imagine him going through another nightmare as intense as last nights or avoiding sleep altogether.

"Again, Boone, along with the rest of you could go to the ranch for a few days and experience life on the other side." Layne's offer would solve Boone's sleep dilemma for sure. Mena couldn't travel to the other side and neither could her devilment.

"If young Boone is no longer in the house, the witch may target another member of the family. If we alter our regular schedule, we may alert her that plans are being made to eliminate her presence." Aunt Pet tapped a finger on her cheek while deep in thought.

16

"Pet's right. We can't put anyone else in danger. Let's hope we get some helpful information from the church visitation log." Mama set a fresh pot of coffee on the table and served up more cheese and eggs.

"I'll head out for the church after I tend to a couple of chores out at the barn," Daddy said.

"I'll take care of things at the barn, Daddy. I still need to move those calves over to the Miller place so the children can get acquainted with them and start their training." I welcomed some normal activities to take my mind off this witch and her intentions, whatever they may be.

"I'd love to be outside in the fresh air and sunshine, Ms. Lynzi. I'd like to help, too." Boone had been on lockdown for several days and I suspected he experienced a fierce case of cabin fever right about now. His animal side needed to connect with nature and his run in the pre-dawn hours only left him wanting more.

Everyone went their separate ways to take care of the tasks they'd volunteered to complete. A glorious spring morning welcomed us to the barn along with the sounds of the animals.

Boone paused briefly as he gazed at the spot on the floor where his brother had died only hours before. Although Tom and his clan had cleaned the visible reminders, the scene was burned into all our memories. He sucked in a sharp breath and set in to cleaning stalls and feeding the animals in and around the barn. His enthusiasm for the work added to his satisfied expression and said he was settling into his place in life. I recognized that contented air about him. It was the same content feeling I had since I'd found Layne again and we were settling into the life we had both craved for so long.

The calves were loaded onto the trailer after the chores were completed at the Brady barn. Boone drove the truck to the Miller place and backed up to the gate to unload the start of what I hoped would be a long and rewarding experience for the children. He seemed to have a blast introducing the children to their new responsibilities. I watched as he interacted with the children. He was good with them and would make a great father one day. The proof was displayed before me as he helped the children adjust the halters on the calves and taught them how to check the fit and loosen the buckles as the calves grew.

We said our goodbyes to the Millers and drove back to the barn to wash out the trailer and head into the house for a much-needed lunch break. Layne had been close by my side the entire time and although I couldn't see his expression, it was evident in the words spoken close to my ear. He was pleased to have some sense of normalcy back in our lives.

"Boone, the chef is taking requests for lunch. Burgers or salad?" I was relaying the menu since Layne had offered to get lunch started.

"A burger sounds great, Ms. Lynzi." I wasn't surprised the hungry werepanther chose the more carnivorous offerings.

"You heard that, right, chef? And you already know what I like." Layne had stressed to me over and over that I never had to worry about my weight now that I was a part of his world, but old habits are hard to break, and I considered salads to be healthy eating anyway. He, in turn, whispered some mighty enticing afternoon intentions in my ear as he faded away to the house to start the grill.

"The trailer's all cleaned out and unhitched, Ms. Lynzi. Do you want me to move the truck up to the house?"

"I'll move it, Boone. I need to get my bag and the stock log. You go on in and get washed up. I have a feeling those medium rare burgers are just about done." I was ready to wash off some barn dust, get a cold glass of tea, and dive into a salad myself.

"Yes, Ma'am. I think can hear a couple of cheeseburgers calling my name." He hurried off toward the house with a happiness I had not seen often since he reintroduced himself last week. He wore it well.

I climbed into the cab of the pick-up, gathered my stock log and other receipts I needed to file away for tax purposes, and drove the truck up to the house. The wisteria was in full bloom and hanging like clusters of grapes from the tall pine trees by the drive. Peach, yellow, and purple iris blossoms stood on erect stems along the fence. Spring had unfolded into a colorful wonder, an artist's pallet.

I paused a moment to soak in the beauty as if I needed another reason to be happy. The wedding was in a couple of days. I'd be perfectly happy with a garden wedding here at our home or my rose garden back at the ranch on the other side but since Layne couldn't be seen here, I'd be a sight walking down the aisle, and standing in front of the preacher all by myself. Texas was a good choice, and the wedding planners would make sure there was an abundance of spring flowers.

A slight rumble in my tummy brought me from my wedding daydreams and reminded me lunch was waiting inside for me. I slid from the seat and leaned back in to collect my bag. As I turned to close the truck door, I caught sight of a woman stomping around the corner of the house toward me. "Hey, I'm Lynzi. Can I help you?"

As she came closer, I noticed a *less than pleased* expression etched onto her face. "Are you the witch who lives here? The one who killed my Del?"

"Now, wait just a minute. First, I am *not* a witch and second, I *did not* kill Del. Now, if you'd care to come inside, we could discuss what really happened."

"Nooo!" she screamed as she lunged toward me with both hands formed into claws ready to rip the skin from my body.

17

I drew the truck door as close to me as I could get it and waited for the perfect moment. I shoved it open with all the force I had to meet my attacker head on. With a loud thud, she bounced back and fell hard on her rump.

Thinking *that* reality check would take some of the fight out of her, I stepped from behind the door. It was only hopeful thinking though since she scrambled to her feet and came at me a second time. She made contact this time by squsszing both hands around my neck all the while chanting some strange words. Gasping for air, I grabbed hold of her wrists and broke the hold as I spotted Boone tearing out the back door toward us. She swung a fist, and I reached up with my forearm to block the blow.

A familiar hand latched onto my waist and tugged me out of the reach of the crazed woman. The loud smack I heard but did not see delivered caused her to fly backward and land on her backside again. I straightened myself, my hands balled into tight fists. She had to believe I had delivered the blow. Layne's identity could never be discovered.

Boone took his protective stance in front of me. "Mena, what are you doing here? Ms. Lynzi didn't kill Del. He was executed by panther law for everything he did to me and Jesse and Mama."

The crazy witch resembled a human crab scooting backward on her hands and feet, trying to stand, and regain her senses. I could almost see the steam coming from her ears she was so mad.

"You didn't lift a finger to help poor Del and now you've thrown in with *this* witch. You *will* pay for what you did, Boone Weaver." She raised her hand and started to speak in riddles again as if to cast another spell of some sort on Boone.

I moved around Boone with my shadow still covering my back. "This is your only warning, Mena. Leave this place and leave us in peace. Keep messing with me and my family and I *will* come after you." I raised my arm with my fist still clenched to emphasize my point. Layne accentuated my declaration with a gust of wind powerful enough to knock her on her butt, yet again.

"I'll get you. I don't know what kind of witch you are but I'll get you. And Boone, you only tasted the beginning. You'll wish you were dead before I'm done with you. Careful what you dream, it might come true." She scrambled to her feet and ran around the corner of the house and to the car she had left parked out on the side of the road.

"Lynzi. Are you hurt?" Layne was hovering again.

"Ms. Lynzi, did she hurt you?" Boone, too.

I blew out a breath. "Whew. You both worry too much. I'm fine. Not a hair out of place." I shook my ponytail. "Which is more than I can say for Mena." A confident grin spread across my face as I raised my left fist and revealed my prize. Several dozen strands of frizzy, bleached blond hair had been captured in my scuffle with the witch. "Ooo, she's in bad need of a touch up, too. Gray roots." I made a face as I examined my reward and wondered if we now had everything, we needed to do the job of eliminating Mena from our lives.

Layne's hands clasped onto my waist, he lifted and spun me around in midair. After my feet were back on the ground, I propped my hands on my hips. "Layne Brady, what if someone saw that? People don't just fly around their backyards on their own. At least not here."

"Hey, you already got the reputation as a scary ol' witch, so why not?" He chuckled as he took my hand and led me into the house.

"Sounds reasonable to me," Boone chimed in.

"You two best be careful with those smart mouths. I'll take my broomstick to the both of you."

After lunch, we got word that Daddy was home from his visit with the preacher. Now, it was time for another strategy meeting and to let everyone in on the news of our latest acquisition. Did I dare hope our witch problem *would* be solved tonight?

Our planning team had reassembled at the table. Mama sliced a homemade pound cake and whipped some fresh cream. Aunt Pet brought sweet strawberries from the gardens on the other side. Iced tea and strawberry shortcake on a warm spring afternoon was hard to beat and as we enjoyed our dessert, we shared our latest adventure.

I withdrew a plastic sandwich bag from my pocket with our treasure zipped inside and plopped it down on the table. Everyone stared. Mostly confused but then Mama guessed the contents and asked the question to confirm her thoughts. "Is that what I think it is?"

"If you think it's Mena's hair, then yes, it *is* what you think it is." Layne announced with pride ringing in his voice. "My little lynx collected it in her latest scrap."

"Hey, she started it. I just let her *think* I finished it. So can we fill the bottle now and set our witch trap?" I was eager to get on with this.

"There is nothing standing in our way now, little one. We can complete the filling of the bottle, activate the spell, and wait for Mena to invade Boone's dreams tonight." Aunt Pet was self-assured and cool as a cucumber and *that* was good enough for me.

"I'm afraid there's more coming tonight than last night. She was awful riled up when she hightailed it out of there this afternoon." Boone summed up my thoughts as well. We had all assumed tonight would be an exact repeat of last light. If, in fact, she had targeted both Boone and me, we were both in danger.

"Yes, young Boone, you are correct. This witch revealed much about herself with her actions this day. We must expect the unexpected from her tonight." Aunt Pet was cautious and deep in thought.

"Do we need *two* witch bottles, Pet?" Mama asked. "One to keep near Boone and another one near Lynzi? We have enough ingredients for two."

"We won't need two if Lynzi's not here." Layne crossed his arms over his chest, set a determined jaw, and raised an eyebrow as if the problem was solved and he'd had the solution all along.

"I'm not afraid of the likes of her, *much*. But I'm still not running away." I crossed my arms and glared right back at him. It was a standoff, of sorts.

"We still don't know what she's capable of Lynzi. Please, try and be reasonable." His eyes searched mine, pleading for me to go along with him.

"One bottle will be sufficient for our needs. Young Boone will sleep tonight as usual and as the witch invades his dreams again, she will be no more." Aunt Pet delivered the instructions for tonight. "If she has any idea, she will harm our little one, it will be necessary for her to reevaluate her thought process." She turned toward me with an assured air. "The wards I have spun around you and your bedroom are strong enough to keep this witch and her entire coven away. Should she attempt to gain entry to your room, her efforts will be halted. She will not be surprised as she already sees you as a witch."

"That is good news, Aunt Pet. Thank you. But I am concerned her family will retaliate when they find she's gone." I prayed our current situation would be resolved soon and that we wouldn't make the situation worse.

Daddy scraped the last spoonful of whipped cream and strawberries from his bowl. "We may not have to worry about any witches beyond this crazy Mena. According to the preacher, he visits the house on Sawmill Road quite often and says the ladies there are peaceable folk with no intentions of harming anyone. They had mentioned a cousin visiting for a week or so but said she's gone now. He got the message they were glad to see her move on." Daddy added his findings to the mix. At least it sounded as if eliminating Mena wouldn't bring her family down on us, and that *was* reassuring news.

"So, we're dealing with a solitary witch, with revenge on her mind, and the wedding is Saturday." I worried my bottom lip between my teeth.

"Do not worry so, my little one. We will put an end to her this night. Everything is set in Texas and your wedding will be beautiful."

Aunt Pet seemed as excited about the wedding as Layne and I. Mercy, let this latest situation come to an end tonight.

We put off bedtime as long as possible. No one wanted Boone to go through another terrifying nightmare but shortly after midnight, we decided to fill our witch trap and put it to the test.

After the coffee mugs and playing cards were cleared from the kitchen table, we gathered the witch bottle, and the magical ingredients. Aunt Pet filled the bottle about half full of wine and selected a long sprig of fresh rosemary. She inserted into the neck of the bottle where the herb curled inside a couple of times and came to rest near the bottom. Pins and needles were dropped in next and settled about the leaves on the rosemary stem.

Aunt Pet wound a few strands of Mena's hair around another twig of the herb and added it to the container. Additional pins and needles layered in the witch bottle completed our trap. She added more wine leaving an inch or so of headspace and sat back with a satisfied air about her.

Everyone watched the glass container in silence until Daddy spoke, "Don't you need to *say* something, or wave your hands over it, or *something* Pet?" He studied the bottle, expecting a magic wand to be required maybe?

"The magic has been silent in the bottle for many years. Now that the ingredients are combined, the spell is active and waiting for our trouble making witch to appear."

"Huh, just like adding eggs and milk to a mix to make a cake." Mama summed it up.

"Yes, yes, our trap is ready."

Everyone turned toward Boone to gauge his reaction.

Boone inhaled a sharp breath. "Let's do this," he exhaled as he took the bottle and cork in his hand and stood to leave the room.

Layne reached out to clasp Boone's shoulder. "Boone, would you like help getting to sleep? Maybe another happy dream to dream? We're not even sure she'll show tonight."

Boone nodded, pleased at the thought. His tone had softened and become peaceful this morning when he related his memory of the pleasant dream from last night. The idea of a wife and children, his own family, had pleased him, and the thought of going back to his dream home brought a sparkle to his eyes. I could relate. Layne had introduced me to his new life and world through a series of dreams, each more perfect than the last, and my desire to revisit his world had been forever on my mind.

We followed him upstairs to his room. He placed the witch bottle on the dresser behind a figurine to conceal it somewhat from sight and put the cork on the bedside table within handy reach.

I said my goodnights and stepped to the door, out of Layne's way. Boone stretched out on the bed and rested his head on the pillow. Layne placed his thumb in the center of Boone's forehead as he closed his eyes. His dream would begin soon. I prayed the witch bottle would work and there would be no more nightmares.

Layne and I crossed the hall to our room. A concerned look covered his face as he closed the door.

"Don't worry. This is going to work. I can feel it in my bones." I slid my arms around his waist filling them with my warm security blanket.

He turned to lock the door and envelope me in his embrace. "Why don't we go to the ranch for a few hours?"

"You know we need to be here, for Boone. What's gonna happen when Mena comes for him tonight? He may need us. And you know the wards Aunt Pet placed around the room are strong. I am safe, Layne."

He pressed closer and snuggled down into the curve of my neck. "You realize while I have you trapped in my love lock, I could just whisk you away somewhere, anywhere in the world, right? A secluded beach in Florida, a café in Paris, the North Pole—" He lifted me off the floor and twirled us around and around the room.

"I would hope you wouldn't do that after I asked you not to. And besides, I'm wearing your T-shirt, and no underwear."

He stepped back and gazed at me, mouth opened, and wide eyed in surprise. "Then I'll have to be careful where we go. Close your eyes," he said and quickly pressed my head to his chest in a rush.

Everything went dark.

18

When my head stopped spinning, I opened my eyes. I was furious that Layne had zipped us away to . . . "You stinker." Another survey of my surroundings revealed he had transported us across the room and into our own bed.

"What?" he asked, his eyes bright with excitement, and a *gotcha* grin spreading across his sweet lips. "It would've taken *way* too long to *walk* the entire distance from the door." He leaned down and rubbed the tips of our noses together.

"Thank you for staying here. I want to be near if Boone needs us."

"I know mother hen. You have that protection drive but so do I. And just to be clear, if I thought for a split-second Aunt Pet's wards weren't strong enough to keep you safe, you *would not* be here." Layne extended a playful finger and caressed the outline of my lips. His expression confirmed he was serious, and I wasn't about to start an argument over protecting your loved ones. I exhaled as the corners of my mouth lifted softly. I snuggled down into the arms of the man who adored me and understood me completely.

Sleep eluded me as I wrestled with thoughts of Mena and what she had up her sleeve for Boone's dreams tonight. I wanted to find her and stuff her crazy butt into that bottle with my bare hands, but since that had to be left to the magic, I contained my urges on the subject.

Layne picked right up on my state of unrest. "She may not even show up tonight. Would you be agreeable to a short dream trip? We'll physically be here and hear him if he calls out."

"I would love to see Trigger and the piglets. Can we dream about the barn at the ranch?"

A sweet smile spread across his lips as his eyes widened. "Anything you want, darlin'," he whispered as he kissed the tip of my nose and settled his thumb on the center of my forehead.

I OPENED MY EYES TO three curious faces gazing down at me. My little Monkey, Pooh, and Buddy grunted their welcome. I found Layne and I were still in the same snuggle position but now in a bed of hay in the piglet's stall. "Hey there, y'all."

We shifted ourselves into a sitting position, leaned back against the stall wall, and welcomed the piggies as they insisted that they snuggle with us. I inhaled deeply. "Why do I feel such complete peace here even after all that's happened?" Monkey flopped across my lap and rolled to her side to get her belly rubbed.

"Well, we know Aunt Pet has everything protected here. There's peace in safety. You know I would protect you to the very end. This is your home, and home is a safe place. Take your pick." He reached out and tugged Buddy onto his lap.

"Mmm, all the above. I have never been so safe and protected. Oh, as a child, I had this same sense of security at home with my family, but not so much in my adult life. This *is* my home. This is where I belong."

Pooh nudged my hand to remind me she was ready for some attention. "Oh, okay, it's your turn, huh?"

We laughed as Buddy grunted his satisfaction with attention he received. I leaned my head on Layne's shoulder and listened to the happy sounds of my piglets sleeping on our laps.

A gentle wind wafted through the double doors opened at both ends of the barn. The sunlight spilled in and danced on the floor as the limbs of the giant pecan trees outside swayed in the breeze. Such calm. Such peace. My eyelids became heavy as I watched the back-and-forth movements but before I drifted off to sleep the sunlight faded, hidden behind what I assumed was a cloud.

The barn dimmed at an unusual rate. The dark cloud crept closer to the door, inching its way inside, and toward the stall we occupied. I turned to Layne who was already on high alert. He put a finger to his lips to caution me to be silent. We watched the cloud roll into the barn and inch its way closer mimicking a live creature.

Layne placed a hand on my shoulder.

"DARLIN', WAKE UP. SHE'S here," he whispered.

I opened my eyes. No barn. No dark cloud closing in on us. We were in our bed.

He gave me a tiny shake and repeated his warning as he slid from the bed and eased into his jeans. "She's in the house."

I stood quietly and slipped on my shorts under my T-shirt. I wanted to be dressed in case this visit prompted a fast get away courtesy of my fiancé and travel agent.

Layne waited by the door and listened for sounds from across the hall. We could hear Boone moaning slightly, gently tossing and turning but nothing indicated a nightmare had invaded his dreams.

"What did you give him to dream?"

"Same as before. Wife, family, and home." He leaned closer to decide if the time was right to go in.

More soft moaning and stirring. "Doesn't sound like a nightmare. What if he's dreaming, they're you know, having a private moment?"

Layne's lips curled upward, he raised a fist in a victory signal and whispered, "Yes! Score one for Boone." He chuckled and leaned down for a soft kiss. "But Mena *is* there. The dream world is close knit, darlin'. We saw her coming in our dream."

"No, Mena. No more. Leave my family alone!" Boone bellowed out the command. His words confirmed he was not having a pleasant dream, and that Mena was with him mentally if not physically in his room. Three creaks of the floorboards from across the hall confirmed he was out of bed and walking across the floor.

We crept into the hallway and over to Boone's room. Layne eased the door open, allowing us a peek inside.

He stood at the foot of his bed pointing toward the dresser and the witch bottle hidden there. "Leave!" he commanded the shadowy form stationed by the window.

Mena threw her head back and laughed. "Did I interrupt your sweet dream, Boone? Well, get used to it. It only gets worse. Every night I will get closer to taking everything from you just like you took everything from me. I will *squeeze* the life out of that little girl and that pretty, blond wife you were dreaming about. You *will* suffer Boone Weaver." She screeched her intentions at the top of her lungs.

Boone moved his arm to point at the intruder by the window. "Never! You will *never* get to them. I'll see you dead and burning in hell first, Mena." Boone's body began to shake. His arm and hand remained rigid, pointing directly at the witch.

The room started to vibrate and sent the bottle on the dresser to dance.

"Go!" Another command thundered toward the witch.

A thin blue spark of electric energy zigzagged from his fingertip and hit the witch, slamming her against the wall. She shrieked in pain as her entire body began to shudder out of control, sending the blue streak ricocheting around the room.

Layne leapt aside, jerking me out of the line of fire but not before the magical charge nicked my upper arm causing an electric tingle.

Boone moved his finger in the direction of the bottle as her body began to contort and dissolve into a dark haze. Her vaporized form followed the path his finger commanded. A spiraling stream of black mist circled the bottle before it entered the neck, swirled inside, and became tangled among the nest of pins and needles resting on the rosemary. Now, fully consumed inside the bottle.

Boone watched the mixture swirl in the bottle for a moment before he retrieved the cork from the bedside table and moved to the dresser. He peered into the bottle at the mix of witch and wine. His left hand steadied the bottle while he pressed the cork tight into the opening.

"Boone, are you alright?" Layne asked after a few moments of silence.

"She's gone. She's trapped in the bottle just like Aunt Pet said she would be." He didn't take his eyes off the witch's glass confines. The essence that was once Mena still stirred inside in an agitated motion.

"Looks that way. How do you feel? That was a bit more than the bottle's magic at work just now. Has that ever happened before?" Layne asked.

We both were concerned for Boone and his state of mind. He remained motionless. I wondered how he would handle all this. More death and in such a short span of time.

At last, he spoke. "No. Never. I had no idea I had any magical ability until Aunt Pet mentioned it, and I sure never felt anything that powerful before." He inhaled, filling his lungs before he continued. "How do I feel now? I feel . . . like lightin' a big ol' fire. Layne?"

We both blew out a relieved breath.

"Well, get your britches on and meet us out back." Layne laughed and headed into the hallway. Neither of us had to be asked twice if we were ready to put an end to this whole vengeful witch business.

In anticipation of our witch bottle trap working, the men had stacked firewood, bonfire style, at the far side of the backyard and doused it with charcoal lighter fluid to allow it to soak into the logs. We'd only had a few hours' sleep, but the entire family filed out into the yard to see this plan through to completion.

Layne added another generous amount of charcoal starter and stepped back to allow Boone enough room to toss a match at the base of the stack. This was his nightmare to end. I prayed this would bring about the closure he needed to put all this behind him and be able to move on with his life. He deserved to be happy.

He took out a couple of matches and closed the box as he studied the stack of wood. The tips of the matches sparked as he dragged them against the strike zone and ignited a slight flash to the ends of the wooden sticks. After they burned steady, he tossed them onto the woodpile.

With a loud *whoosh*, the fire raged forth and reached heights of eight feet before the blaze settled. We waited for all the wood to become fully involved so there'd be no doubt it would continue to burn and get the job done.

Boone turned to the magical expert and asked, "Aunt Pet? Is it time? I don't want to jump the gun on this and mess everything all up."

"It is time, young Boone."

Boone glanced around at the other members of the family before he set his focus on the bottled in his hand. Locating the center and hottest spot in the blaze, he tossed the bottle into the flames.

We all took a couple of steps back in anticipation of an expected explosion. In a few short minutes, the intense heat raised the temperature of the wine inside the corked bottle to the boiling point. Small bubbles formed and moved in a rapid motion causing the bottle to jiggle about. It jumped in the flames several times before it exploded into tiny pieces. The wine sizzled and the rosemary seared to a crisp along with the strands of Mena's hair and all her evil intentions. Everyone remained silent as the heat melted the bottle shards and Mena was gone.

Hours remained before the inferno would burn itself out. Mama and Daddy along with Aunt Pet decided to return to their rooms and get a few more hours of sleep.

We grabbed some of the heavy wooden lawn chairs and stretched out to enjoy the night sky and the roaring fire before us.

"I can't believe it's all over." Boone stared into the fire. "I keep expecting her to rise up out of the flames spoutin' off some more about *me* ruining *her* life."

"I understand your fear, Boone, but Aunt Pet has been around for, well, for hundreds of years learning about all kinds of magic. I trust her, but believe me, I do understand you wanting to be careful," Layne said, reassuring him.

I had snuggled in the chair with Layne and closed my eyes. From the tone of the conversation going on, I gathered some male bonding was about to take place, so I kept still and let nature take its course.

"Was it *just* a dream, Layne, or did I see my actual future? Is she real? Am I ever going to have a home and a family of my own?" Boone had some of the same questions about the Fae dream making ability as did I a few weeks back.

"I have no doubt you'll have a home, a wife, and children someday, Boone. The dreams are inside you. I just gave them a nudge so you would realize how good life can be. Do I know her name or where she lives? Can I tell you the exact day you'll meet her? No, I'm afraid I can't see into the future or read fortunes. But she *is* out there, and when you meet her, you'll know it." He brushed my cheek before he continued. "There's something, call it fate, call it instincts, if you will, but something special in us as preternatural beings that tugs at our heart and lets us know when we've met *the* one. It doesn't guarantee smooth sailing but even through the storms, the end result is a lifetime of happiness."

"I reckon I best get busy findin' a place of my own if I expect to start a family soon."

I eased my eyes open a bit and caught sight of Layne watching the fire. He glanced down, kissed the air in my direction, and winked at me. Our life was going to be perfect and so would Boone's. One day.

After daylight, I stirred in Layne's arms. "Is it over? Has the wicked witch melted?" He shifted his weight to a better sitting position.

I yawned and stretched up. My arm ached. The sting from Boone's electric zinger, along with the cramped position I had put myself in caused my arm to throb. I massaged it a bit to ease the pain.

"You okay, sweetheart?"

"Yeah. My arm still tingles a bit from the lightning bolt in Boone's room earlier but I'm fine."

"Sorry about that, Ms. Lynzi. I still have no idea where that came from or what it was exactly." Boone poked around in the embers with a stick to determine if any sign of the witch trap had survived the blaze. "I can't find a speck of that bottle left here but I'm tempted to put a few more logs on the coals and start it up again to be sure."

"I can't say I don't agree with your logic. Better safe than sorry I always say." I stared into the remains of our bonfire praying our problem had been solved and the world had one less evil, vengeful creature to haunt and terrorize people.

Aunt Pet appeared on the scene along with Layne's parents each carrying a tray with breakfast foods. "The witch ceased to exist as soon as the bottle exploded. We are free of her and her evil intentions." Aunt Pet reassured us as she eased the tray containing the table settings, jelly, and mustard on the table. Mama and Daddy added trays of sausage biscuits, juice, and coffee.

"This is so sweet, but we could have come inside to eat. Y'all didn't have to bring it out here to us." I passed around the napkins and poured coffee. We waited for Daddy to ask blessings on the food and our family before we dug in.

"We thought some fresh air would do us all good," Mama said as she smiled and absorbed the early spring morning. Her voice had a manner of relief to it. A load had been lifted from her shoulders as well.

"Most important, we need to finalize travel plans for today or tomorrow," Aunt Pet said.

I realized after a moment's thought that we had *finally* made it to Friday and the day before our wedding. I gazed at the beauty of the blue, morning sky with wonder. "Oh my, we made it. Against more of the strangest odds, we made it."

"Yes, we did. Now we need to decide when we leave for the penthouse." Layne beamed as he snagged another sausage biscuit and dressed it with a squirt of yellow mustard.

"That would depend on how much set up still needs to be done. I'm ready now if there's anything I can to do to help." I had been told everything was under control every time I'd asked if I could help in the past few weeks, and I expected to hear the same answer now. We had whisked away to Texas several times for wedding dress fittings until we decided on a simple white satin with a lavender organza overlay.

Some of the suggestions had been far more glamorous than I was comfortable wearing. As far as I was concerned, jeans and a T-shirt with everyone gathered in the barn would have been a perfect wedding but this was a family affair and if it made everyone happy to see me all dressed up then, so be it. Let everyone have their fun, it would be beautiful, and I'd have a happy family.

"All tasks have been completed. We are only missing the bride and groom," Aunt Pet assured us.

Still unable to comprehend, I shook my head. "Then I say we leave right after breakfast if everyone else is agreeable."

"I want you folks to rest easy everything will be tended to while y'all are gone." Boone smiled and offered his help.

"But, Boone, you're part of the family now. We want you to come with us and be part of the celebration. It'll be fun and you certainly deserve some fun after all you've been through. What do you say?" I hadn't extended an invitation before now. I had assumed all along he would come with us.

His eyes searched the air around him for an answer before his gaze settled on his lap. "Ms. Lynzi, I came here without a stitch of clothes. I'm only dressed now because you all have been so kind." He paused and scratched his head. "I . . . need to find a job and start making my own way. Now, Mr. Brady, I still intend to work here for you to help cover some of your losses just like I promised."

Layne shot a quick glance and a wink in my direction. I had no mind reading abilities, but his message was loud and clear.

"Boone, you're right. You do need to make your own way. Lynzi and I are going to need someone to look after our place while we're away on our honeymoon. You could stay at our house, and you'd be close enough to Daddy to help out here, too. So, you have a job if you want it and it would mean a lot to Lynzi and me . . . to all of us, if you'd agree to come to the wedding." Layne extended an invitation I prayed Boone would see as a solution to his dilemma of getting his life back on track. "There will be an advance in your salary so you could go shopping for your own clothes and personal items as soon as we get to Texas." Layne paused to allow him to absorb the offer.

Boone huffed out a breath and shook his head. A pleased, relieved air surrounded him. "I couldn't ask for anything to be more perfect, Layne. Ms. Lynzi, I'd really like to go to your wedding."

"Then it's settled. We leave for Texas right after breakfast." I took a liking to this boy the first time I met him and now I counted him as part of my family.

"Now, that's what I'm talking about," Daddy said as he poured another round of coffee.

Breakfast conversation became livelier and more upbeat than it had been in days. Life was good. We talked our plans for after the honeymoon that included relaxation and spending time with family. Oh, sure, there'd be lots of hard work with the cattle here, and the animals at the ranch on the other side but those jobs are labors of love and I'd be laboring right alongside my family and the love of my life.

After the breakfast dishes were done and bags were packed, we all stood in the living room ready to make the trip to Texas.

Lake and Woods had popped in to assist with the travel arrangements.

"See you all in a minute," I called as Layne cradled me to his chest.

A stabbing pain shot through my arm. I winced and grabbed hold of the source of my discomfort. My smile faded. The happy, ecstatic feeling drained from my entire body. A dark cloud surrounded me, and I stepped out of Layne's arms. Reality had set in.

"Lynzi? What's wrong?" Layne asked with a puzzled expression.

"Everything." I searched the faces of the people in the room. Puzzled. Confused.

"Everything? Like what honey?"

Confusion engulfed me. What was I thinking? "This whole crazy life. The light bulb has finally come on. Being with you has been one disaster after another. I can't live like this. Always looking over my shoulder for the latest insane person trying to kill me. Mena may be gone, but Allvis is still gunning for me. Who else wants to kill me?" I shook my head. "I've had enough." I turned and walked away, out the back door, and climbed into my truck. I had to put some distance between myself, and this magical existence that had threatened on so many occasions to end my life. It was over.

19

The truck came to a stop in front of my old house. I still maintained a presence here for my girls when they came for a visit. This was their home, the place where they were raised. It would always be open for them. Their rooms were just as they had left them.

This magic business wasn't for me. I had to get back to a normal, regular existence.

I busied myself in the kitchen. Coffee was normal. I'd make coffee. The rich, dark liquid trickled into the pot. This is the way life should be. Normal. Uncomplicated. Safe. I wouldn't have to constantly look over my shoulder for any crazies trying to harm me. Normal.

I found my favorite old mug with the rooster on it, filled it with my steamy brew, punched a couple of holes in the top of a can of cream, and watched as the white liquid swirled around the interior of the mug to mix with the coffee creating a warm, soothing drink to relax me.

My recliner welcomed me as I sank into the center, leaned my head back, and stared up at the ceiling. I was at peace. Finally. Peace.

A group of folks appeared in the corner of my living room but remained cautiously quiet. Maybe if I ignore them, they'll go away.

"Lynzi? Honey."

I lifted my cup to my lips and sipped the smooth, warm liquid. My eyelids eased shut as I savored the flavor. *If I don't acknowledge his presence . . .*

"Aunt Pet, what's happening? This is not Lynzi."

Who the hell do you think it is, genius?

"I sense magic at work inside our little one. Confusing her grasp on reality."

There she goes, 'sensing' again. Give it a rest, old girl.

"Mena? But she's dead. How could she be controlling Ms. Lynzi now?"

Oh, no, Boone. Not you, too. Why don't you go catch a mouse, kitty cat?

"It is not the dead witch, young Boone. This is a backlash of the magic you added to force the evil one into the bottle."

"*I*, did this to Ms. Lynzi? Oh, Layne. I didn't know. I'm so sorry. I—"

Sorry for what, kid? Showing me the light? You deserve a medal, if you ask me.

"That blue streak of energy that shot from Boone's finger and bounced around the room this morning . . . it did touch her arm, come to think of it. Aunt Pet? Do you mean . . . *that's* what's causing this change in her?"

"Layne. Aunt Pet. What have I done? I never intended to hurt Ms. Lynzi."

But you did open my eyes and set me free, kid. Thanks for that!

"You have yet to learn your potential, young Boone. It will come in time and with practice."

"That's all well and good, Aunt Pet, but what do we do now? Can you fix this?" Layne *sounded* concerned.

"It is the magic of young Boone. He is the only one who can reverse the process."

How 'bout y'all reverse yourselves right out of my living room, and my life.

"*My* magic? But I don't even know what I did, so how can I *undo* it? Please tell me how? I want to fix this. Make it right."

This is getting real old, real fast. I need more coffee. I carried my mug to the kitchen for a refill.

"Aunt Pet, can't *you* undo this and get Lynzi back to me?"

"Young Boone must focus and concentrate on reversing the action."

"Boone, concentrate on Lynzi the way she was this morning."

Boone sucked in a sharp breath and held it. His brow knit together, and lips pursed tight to try and follow the directions he'd been given.

Seriously? Squinting your eyes and grunting is your idea of making magic? Kinda looks like a bad stomach bug to me.

He whooshed out the breath he held. "Nothing. Layne, I scared I'm gonna, break her, or somethin'."

"Try again, Boone. Try, pointing at her. That's where your electric charge came from this morning."

May as well save their energy. I'm fine. I don't need fixing.

Boone took in another breath and started squinting and grunting again.

You keep that straining up and this could get ugly.

At least it produced some results this time. A blue streak, same as this morning, crackled from his fingertip, and bounced off the walls. A tiny explosion on the coffee table sent slivers of several figurines shooting around the room.

And there goes that ceramic duck into a dozen pieces. Oh well, I never liked the darn thing anyway, but he needs to stop before he breaks something I do like.

"Boone, you're gettin' there. Concentrate harder," Layne urged.

Here we go again. I need a camera. This is hilarious.

The thin blue streak of electric energy zigzagged from the tip of his finger again and bounced from wall to wall, floor to ceiling before it hit me smack dab in the middle of my forehead, causing me to take a couple of steps backward. Coffee splashed down the front of my shirt.

Now that *pissed me off!*

I steadied myself and gave my head a good shake to gather my senses, ready to lay into the trio of busybodies for even being in my house just as Layne reached for me.

"Get your hands off me." I jerked my arm away, stepped out of his reach, and searched the area around me. My kitchen. My old house. What the——? "Layne? I thought we were going to Texas. What changed? Why are we here? And why am I drenched in coffee?"

Layne rushed forward and gathered me into his arms. "Lynzi. I've never been so scared in my whole life." He held me tight. Like he hadn't seen me in forever.

"Why? What happened?"

"Honey, we think you got caught in the crossfire this morning when Boone put Mena in the bottle."

"Crossfire?" I searched the memories from the capture and disposal of Mena. Nothing out of the ordinary, well except for the whole unbelievable turn of events. "Mercy, Layne. What in the world are you talking about?"

"The witch fought back and tried to use her own magic to avoid capture in the bottle. Her last effort was to zap away Boone's happiness. Aunt Pet's pretty sure you got a portion of the magic she intended for Boone. A reversal spell intended to wipe away his desire for happiness."

"She did, however, underestimate the strength of young Boone's powers."

Boone stood as if his feet were glued to the floor. His arm remained in a raised position with his trigger finger extended. "Ms. Lynzi. I'm so sorry. I wouldn't hurt you for the world."

The spot on my upper arm that had been tagged by the supercharged electrical streak still stung a bit, but it was far from Boone's fault. I certainly would never blame him for any of this witch business. "Boone, you are more a victim here than any of us. None of this is your fault." I pressed his hand down to his side and gave him a little hug of reassurance.

There was no doubt about it. Dead or not, that witch had left her mark. Was this truly the end of her and her vengeful magic? Could I expect any relapses?

20

I t took some convincing from Aunt Pet and me before Layne agreed to continue with our travel plans. His overprotective side was in high gear after the complete turnabout I took from the spell Mena intended for Boone.

We arrived in the living room in the penthouse in San Antonio. It resembled a massive flower garden. Gardenias and lavender roses adorned the tables both inside and outside on the balcony. Gardenia garlands, white candles, and light airy satin and lace drapes hung from the ceiling along all the walls. A buffet table delighted the guard teams, as did the fountain flowing with wine from the ranch.

"Lynzi! Layne! You made it." Cloi bubbled as she hurried in our direction. She had to be the absolute best party planner ever. The decorations, the food, and the wine was all perfect. "I've got all the clothes you picked out in your suite so as soon as you all are ready, we can begin the celebration. Everyone will be here this afternoon. There are tons of gifts for you to open, the food is ready so let's get this party started!"

"You all have done so much work. Look at this place. Everything is so beautiful." I was amazed as I glanced around the room. It had been transformed from an elegant penthouse living area to a bridal fantasy. All our family from the ranch had gathered for our arrival. Mama, Daddy, and all the guards waited for me to drink in the dream world created in celebration of our wedding. I made my way around the room and thanked everyone for their part in making our dream wedding a reality.

The Brady's luggage still sat where it landed earlier, and Boone appeared a bit lost. "I think we need to get everyone settled in their rooms first and I'd like to change. Lake, can I see you in the kitchen for a minute please?"

Layne hooked an arm around my waist and hoisted me to his chest, lifting me off the floor, and turning a full circle. "Mmm-mmm, I do like me a take charge woman."

"Oh, really? Well sir, let's see if you can get Boone and your mama and daddy settled in their rooms while I speak with Lake, then meet me in our room in a few minutes. There's so much I need done and so little time to do it."

"Yes, ma'am. I can do that, but you remember we are *never* short on time. We've got forever." He trailed kisses from the base of my neck to my earlobe causing the inevitable moan to slip passed my lips.

"Uh, umm."

The accentuated sound came from the kitchen and reminded me I had asked Lake to meet me there. "Um, I think I'd better take care of my business with Lake. Do we still have a date in our room in a few minutes?"

"The sooner the better, sweetheart. You are too good to be true, Lynzi Lancaster."

Reality set in. Our dream of being married was finally coming true. Total amazement grabbed and held me for a moment.

"Uh hum." The sound came from the kitchen again accompanied by muffled chuckles from every corner of the room. We had drifted away into our own world again blanking out everything and everyone around us.

"The entire room is watching us, aren't they?" I asked.

Layne smiled and nodded.

"There's no way to handle this gracefully, is there?"

He moved his head side to side, the same grin spread across his face.

I realized we had stood in our embrace for too long a time.

Layne's head continued its slow side to side movement. "'Fraid not, my darlin'."

I put my thinking cap on. "Now don't you be in such a hurry to give up. Just meet me in the bedroom in a few." My feet still dangled in the air, so I slid down my mountain of man and started for the glass doors behind me. "Lake, what are you waiting for, I said I need to speak with you on the balcony."

He threw his hands up in the air, rolled his eyes, and let out an aggravated growl. "Ugh, and here I *thought* I heard the word *kitchen*." More laughter followed as he closed the glass door for a bit of privacy.

"Sorry. We do tend to get lost in each other sometimes." I admitted as I shrugged.

"*Sometimes*?" He raised a playful brow.

I wrinkled my nose. "A lot?"

He smiled and lowered his gaze to his feet before making direct eye contact with me. "Don't ever feel you need to apologize for being in love, Lynzi. If it ever happens for me . . ." His voice trailed off as if he were thinking of the impossible.

I eased my hand on his arm and gave him a half shake. "It *will* happen for you Lake and believe me when I say it'll be when you *least* expect it." That much I could testify to. I had resigned myself to living life alone. The risk of beginning a new relationship was more than I was willing to take given my history of bad choices. And then Layne breezed back into my life and proved dreams do come true.

"Thanks, Lynzi, you're the best. Layne is a lucky man. Now, how can I help you?"

"You know Boone has been wearing Layne's clothes since he first came to the house that night, right? He wanted to stay and look after all the Brady property while we were here, but Layne offered him a job managing our place while we're on our honeymoon. His offer included an advance so he could go shopping for some things all his own. Could you and the boys take a couple of hours and help him out? It would mean a lot to me. Not to mention give Boone a sense of self-worth."

"Sure, we could. I'll go get him and we can leave right away."

I stood on my tiptoes and kissed his cheek. "You're a good brother, Lake."

His expression softened. "Anything for you, Sis."

Layne emerged from the hallway where the guest suites were located as I stepped back inside. "Everyone's settled in their rooms. You ready to get changed?"

"Sure am. Lake is taking Boone shopping so we should have a couple of hours to kill. Got any ideas?" A sweet, innocent smile accompanied my question.

"Oh, girl, come here." He laughed out loud as he gathered me close and transported us into the bathroom in our suite. Water sprinkled on my back before I opened my eyes. Somewhere along the way, all our clothes had disappeared, and we now stood under the shower. I so hoped my underwear wasn't strewn down the hall to our door. "You did say something about a shower, didn't you, sweetness?" His grin widened as he gazed down at me. "Sometimes I think my heart's gonna bust right out of my chest. It is so full of joy, Lynzi. You make me so happy."

I drank in the adoration staring down at me. My heart echoed the truth he voiced. How could any two people be so blessed? "*Happy* doesn't sound like enough. Words can't express what's in my heart. You *are* my dream come true."

He slid his hands behind my thighs and lifted my body up. I settled my legs around his waist and held tight. Sparks zinged as we made love. The water sprayed over us as we collapsed against the wall. Layne held his position for several minutes before he spoke, "You, okay? Ready to finish our shower?"

"I wish we could stay like this. Close. Warm." I buried my face into the curve of his neck and held on tight.

"Take all the time you need, darlin'. We are in no rush here."

After the fireworks simmered down and we were able to shower and make our way back into the bedroom, we got dressed and joined the others in the living room.

Boone was back from his shopping trip. He looked sharp in his black jeans and western style shirt. He truly beamed with pride. I wondered if he had *ever* been shopping in his life. Confidence covered his face as he and Lake chatted with Cloi and one of her friends.

"Layne?"

"Yeah, darlin'?"

"Have Lake and Cloi ever . . . dated? Seems to me, they'd make a nice couple."

"Well, sweetheart, they are great friends but it's just not in the cards for them as a couple. There's no heart-to-heart connection between them. Believe me, they'd know if there was and then we'd all be aware of the bond." He gave my behind a gentle squeeze to remind me of our *connection*. As if I needed any more reminders. Electricity still shot through my body from our *shower* a while ago.

I studied the group across the room and recalled my experience. Although from a human perspective, I understood. "I know as well as anyone, you can't force love. What about Boone? Does the *were* mate bond work like the Fae, heart to heart?"

"Much like that. *Weres* will recognize their mate sometimes before they set eyes on each other. It's more instinct with them but they do bond for life, that much is similar." He eased me closer and nuzzled my neck.

I wanted so much for Lake and Boone to experience the connection Layne and I had. It was more than a bond. It was forever. Would they be forced to experience all the trials and hardships Layne and I had before it happened for them?

21

"Hey, you two. Are we ready to get this party started?" Cloi motioned to chairs beside the tables overflowing with wedding presents.

"Oh, mercy, did everyone in Texas send a gift?" I envisioned enough toasters and blenders wrapped in the white packages to service the entire state.

The family gathered around as Layne and I took our seats to begin to unwrap the mountain of gifts. Regular interruptions from the doorman with more packages almost defeated any headway we made. I hadn't completed any of the registry information Cloi had gathered for me. I already had everything I needed or ever wanted. Yet, here were multiple place settings of the china patterns that *had* caught my eye. How had my thoughts become common knowledge to everyone who'd sent a gift? My new cousin was perceptive to say the least.

As we opened box after box, Cloi placed the matching pieces together on other tables. Completed sets of, well, everything I even imagined soon displayed before us. Everyone was so sweet to think of us.

"Last one," Cloi sang out as she handed us the final package.

I turned to Layne and blew out a weary breath as I gazed into a pair of eyes filled with love. "Have you ever seen so many gifts in your life?"

"Nothing can compare to the gift I see right now, sweetheart." He leaned down for a kiss. "There will probably be more at the wedding tomorrow, but this looks like the last one for a while. Why don't you do the honors?"

I checked for a card. There wasn't one. "What do you think, another set of candlesticks?"

"I do love seeing your skin glow in candlelight, darlin'." He smiled and waggled his eyebrows.

A tingle zinged through my body at the meaning behind his words. I was reminded it had been hours since I held him in my arms. We were long overdue for some alone time but with the crowd gathered here, I wasn't sure when we would be able to slip away again for a long while. "Then I'll keep my fingers crossed for more candlesticks." I slipped ribbon from the box and discarded the paper on the floor by my chair. Twig had put himself in charge of ribbon collection and paper disposal. He had kept the place neat and tidy as usual.

I eased the box top from the package and froze at the sight of the contents. Cold chills skittered up my spine. "Layne?" The hairs on my arms spiked to attention. My heart pounded in my chest. Fear gripped me like a vise. I gasped and stared in horror at the *gift* inside. A matching pair of iron fireplace pokers engraved with our names, *Lynzi* and *Layne* on the handles. The card attached with a lavender ribbon read, *Best Wishes for a Happy Life Together . . . while it lasts.*

Layne sprang to his feet as he searched with frantic eyes around the room for the source of this danger. The box slid from my lap and clattered to the floor with a thud. The clink of the pokers rang out. The guard's weapons were drawn and they at once formed a protective barrier around us. Everyone was on high alert for the threat behind the iron pokers. The same type that Layne had skewered through Allvis' gut the last time we met.

Since iron is fatal to the Fae, and Layne had shoved the poker through Allvis' body with his gloved hand. We had assumed he was dead. The body disappeared shortly after, and we had not seen or heard from him since. Even though his body was gone, and we were unable to confirm his true death, we could only pray he was dead.

Cloi held a short sword in one hand and her cell phone in the other. She had building security lock down all exits and review the video for the carrier of the package we had just unwrapped. Was it Allvis? Was he alive? Had he been *inside* the building?

No one could recall the package having been delivered. It resembled all the other dozens and dozens of packages that had been arriving every day for the past week.

Aunt Pet, bow and arrow in hand, her keen eye searching the area, assured us the magical protection wards had been activated and were in perfect working order. The entire penthouse was protected.

I sat in stunned silence. A mild state of shock had set in. I thought our life would, at long last, be somewhat *normal.* We would be married, and all the bad times would be in the past. There was only one answer. Allvis was alive and here in Texas *and* on the day before our wedding. What did he have planned? Did he intend to stab both of us with our own personalized fire poker?

I realized a hand was on my arm. I dragged myself out of the fog of confusion and recognized a high level of worry on

Boone's face as he knelt at my side. "Ms. Lynzi, tell me what I can do. I don't know what's going on, only that it's bad, real bad, but I won't let anyone hurt you. I promise." My sweet Boone. The level of determination on his face said he was with us to the end.

I smoothed his hair and brushed his cheek. We had been only casual acquaintances when he worked for my granddaddy years ago, but we had become so close in the past week. The concern on his face was genuine. This boy had a good, caring heart, and would be a friend for life.

"You remember we told you iron is deadly to the Fae if they come in direct contact with it, right?" He nodded and glanced down at the two iron pokers scattered on the floor. "You've heard us mention Layne's cousin Allvis, who has caused so much trouble for the family all his life. He managed to kidnap me from the other side and take me to my house in Cranford a few weeks ago. Layne and the boys tracked us there and a big fight broke out in the living room. He and Allvis squared off to put an end to all the mess that had gone on for years." I took a breath and glanced down at the pokers with our names elegantly engraved into the handles. Was the purpose just to frighten us? Or did he intend to kill us with them?

I looked back at Boone, patiently waiting for me to continue. "The final strike was with the fire poker from the set at my fireplace. We thought for sure Allvis was dead after Layne stabbed him through with the poker." I paused to take a breath and try to settle my nerves. The memory of seeing Allvis die was twofold, one of relief that he was at last out of our lives, *and* the ick factor that a dead person lay crumpled on my living room floor.

"He *was* dead. There was no doubt in my mind. I was shaken up, so Layne took me out of the room for a few minutes to help settle my nerves. When we came back, Allvis' body had disappeared. That left us to wonder if someone had taken him away or if he were somehow still alive and got up and left on his own. We haven't heard or seen anything from him since then and we were hoping and praying he was indeed dead and gone. Other than the people in this room, no one knew how he died."

I motioned to the gift on the floor. "Now that these have appeared, we have to continue to wonder if he left under his own power and is coming after us again or if someone else took his body away and is now going to try to avenge his sorry hide."

"Like another Mena. Crazy for a crazy person." Boone caught on fast. It didn't matter if it were a woman or some other loyal follower or followers. The bottom line being, now we had another insane situation to deal with.

What would we be forced to do now? Cancel the wedding? Go on another hunt for Allvis?

Layne knelt beside Boone on the floor at my feet. "Don't worry, darlin'. This changes nothing. We will be married tomorrow." Had he read my heart, the expression on my face, or both? Try as I might, I couldn't hide my fear and concern.

The guards had faded to other locations around the building to check for intruders. Allvis was smart enough to get in or at least get his package inside, but he wouldn't hang around and wait to be captured or killed.

I stood, gathered the pokers, and repackaged them to prevent any of the Fae members in the room from touching them causing any injury. I made my way to the kitchen and took out more dishes of food from the refrigerator. "The boys will be hungry when they get back. I'm going to make more sandwiches."

Both my new mamas appeared at my side and supported my need to keep busy by working in the kitchen.

"Someone will always be at your side, dear. We won't allow him to take you again. You have my word." Layne's mama said.

My Fae mama sensed my concern. I had been kidnapped on two occasions and worried Allvis had perfected his plan and would come after me again.

"I just wish I had packed my shotgun. I don't take kindly to folks threatening my children." My country mama understood and echoed my own thoughts. I wanted Allvis to disappear forever.

"You two are the best support system a girl could ever have. I love you both." I hugged the two of them. We continued to stack sandwiches on a platter and covered them in plastic wrap to keep them fresh.

Layne and his two dads joined us in the kitchen. "Every second of the video from every security camera has been reviewed. Allvis has not been anywhere in or around this building." He tugged me close and wrapped me in his protective arms.

"I realize we should be extra cautious considering the latest development, but I see no reason to change *any* plans. Security has been tightened around the building and I feel we are all safe. Now, I'd like to dance with my daughter unless you'd like to go first, Will." The melodic quality of my Fae father's voice eased my fears and strengthened my resolve. Allvis would not ruin our wedding.

"You two go ahead, as long as you save a dance for this old farmer, Lynzi gal." Mr. Brady kissed my cheek and took his best girl by the hand to lead her back into the living room where some Texas two-step music played.

My Fae daddy twirled me around on the dance floor at a pace I could hardly match. It had been forever since I had danced and now, I realized I should have practiced a bit.

The boys had returned from rounds and had eased back into party mode. The music ended and I brought the platter of sandwiches to the table as they moved over to fill their plates.

Everyone did the best job possible to keep the atmosphere light and put the impending threat aside for the sake of the wedding, but the worry was on everyone's mind.

"Try not to let it get you down, sweetheart. The guards are going to rotate about every thirty minutes. They'll go to the ranch, get a full night's sleep, make their security checks there, and be back here fully refreshed every half hour." Layne reminded me of the time difference between our worlds. Hours or even days could pass in our Fae world while only a short period of time lapsed here in the human world.

I was happy to hear the guards would return home to rest. I wouldn't want them to tire themselves out looking after me. "That's good. Do you have an update from building security?"

"I thought you promised you wouldn't worry." Layne took my chin between his thumb and crooked finger and raised my head so that our eyes met. "He may not have even been here, but this is the kind of trouble that gives him the upper hand. He can cause everyone strife and hardly lift a finger. Besides, we're not certain *who* delivered the package."

He couldn't fool me with his *cool as a cucumber* façade. I recognized worry in those deep brown eyes. Worry along with concern, love, and desire.

"You're right. Nothing has changed. We don't have his body, so we don't know if he's dead or alive, but who else knew about the poker, Layne?" I searched his eyes for an answer he didn't have and rehashing the obvious would result in no new answers. I inhaled a deep breath. My brain needed the oxygen.

No one, not even the devil himself would stop our dream of being together from coming true. I was determined to take control of my life and support the man I loved. "He will not ruin all Cloi's hard work here. Dance with me, cowboy."

He smiled, slipped his arm around my waist, and twirled us in circles back into the living room. Cloi had invited several of her friends since we had a higher number of male attendees at this pre-wedding bash. Everyone enjoyed the music, the food, and the wine.

Allvis was in the back of everyone's mind, but it didn't show as the laughter rang out around the penthouse. No one could destroy the happiness around us tonight.

22

"**D**early beloved . . ." The minister began our wedding ceremony in the quaint little white church on the outskirts of the city.

The concept of hearts connecting people in a special way still amazed me, but the connection Cloi, Mama, and Aunt Pet had with me was unbelievable. The country setting, family, and close friends in attendance, simple though abundant decorations. All aspects detailed here were exactly what I would have chosen if I had made any of the plans for our wedding on my own.

Cloi, Olive, and Lilly stood with me dressed in lavender versions of my wedding dress with white flower garlands cascading from their hair.

Layne's two dads along with Lake shared the best men duties wearing crisp white shirts and black jackets.

We exchanged traditional vows and gold bands in the Christian portion of our wedding ceremony. Having been raised in the church as a boy, Layne agreed we should include both worlds as we pledged to become one and share the rest of our lives together.

The minister closed his bible and smiled at the two of us before he addressed the congregation. "Before the happy couple is pronounced man and wife, I'm going to step aside for Miss Petunia to bless this union in the heartfelt traditions of the Fae people. Miss Pet, ma'am." He smiled and extended a helping hand to Aunt Pet as she stepped up before us.

Cloi was active in the church here and had explained the existence of the Fae was real and that they were a part of human society. She was afraid the preacher would shun her and the others who wished to worship here but without any hesitation, he welcomed the Fae to be part of the congregation. He held the knowledge of the Fae's existence in confidence to prevent problems from anyone who might not understand. He believed we are all God's children.

Aunt Pet smiled as she spoke to Laynaro and Mr. Brady at Layne's side and the proud mamas seated side by side on the front pew. "The union of our two children has at last come to pass as I was always certain it would." She paused and smiled at the two of us. The sparkle in her eyes told me she had other information of the future and every bit of it would be a wonderful and exciting adventure.

"The power of the earth's elements are present with us today to bless this joining. My little one, your heart is pure, and honest and strong. You are to unite with Layne today as his mate for life. His wife." She paused and glanced to the minister who returned her smile. "Please speak your heart's words to Layne before the elements, our family, and God." She smiled in the minister's direction again. Wait. Was our Aunt Pet making eyes at the preacher? I guess you're never too old to look.

Cloi took charge of my bouquet, smiled, and gave my hand an encouraging squeeze. "You'll do fine," she whispered. She had been my coach on several occasions as I organized the thoughts I would speak to Layne today, words from my heart to his. I worried I would never be able to express the intensity of the love my heart held for him and prayed I didn't get tongue-tied and stumble over the most important words I would ever utter.

I turned to the love of my life, took his hands in mine, and smiled as I gazed at the face of my strong angel, my knight in shining armor, and began to speak. "Layne Brady. I have loved you for all my life it seems. Even when we were apart, my heart never let you go completely. You were always tucked away, waiting with the patience of a saint for our time to be together. Now, your heart is my heart, and I vow to treasure it, and care for it forever." Happy tears gathered in my eyes. The lump growing in my throat made it difficult to speak. I swallowed hard.

Layne brought our entwined hands to his mouth and kissed my fingers one at a time. Electricity zinged through my body from the touch of his lips. Energy filled my heart and soul and gave me the strength to continue without breaking down and blubbering like a baby.

"I promise to make you happy, and I promise I'll try *not* to make you crazy with my many human moods. I will care for our love, and it will care for us. Our love will grow as will our family. You saved me from a lonely life, and I will cherish you forever."

His eyes sparkled as he prepared to speak. He cleared his throat and began his vows to me. "Lynzi Lancaster, my sweet girl, you have grown into a beautiful woman. You are my life, my heart, my very reason for living. I vow to love and protect you forever. To provide a life of happiness and make *all* your dreams come true. All I have is yours. All I am or ever will be is because of you. You saved me from simply existing and I promise to make you proud to call me your husband."

We stood trembling. Our vows had been spoken. Our lives pledged each to the other. We held tight to the hands wearing the symbols of our love, a plain gold band for Layne's finger, and a matching band to accompany my diamond ring.

The preacher moved over to join Aunt Pet. The two of them placed their hands on ours as the preacher said, "What the Lord has joined together, let no man divide." He glanced at her and nodded.

"United by pure hearts, forever, together as one." She blew a kiss of approval toward us.

"Layne, you may kiss your bride." The preacher gave him an encouraging clap on the shoulder.

He held fast to our entwined hands as he leaned down for our first kiss as husband and wife. My heart pounded in my chest. We did it. We were married. We were husband and wife. He leaned back a few centimeters and whispered, "My Lynzi. My Wife."

"Ladies and gentlemen, may we present Mr. and Mrs. Layne Brady." He turned us toward the small congregation gathered for our big day. Sweet fiddle music accompanied us down the aisle and out the front door of the church. A white carriage with six white horses waited to carry us away to the reception, or at least a ways down the road if Layne decided to whisk us back to the penthouse for the post-wedding festivities.

Everyone gathered around and to congratulate us. "You've always been part of our family. We just couldn't tell you that you were." Our human mama hugged me as she expressed her well wishes.

"This is so true, dear. We waited so long to welcome you. Now, the ranch has new life and at last, we have a daughter." Layne's mama stepped closer to her husband to be wrapped in his arms.

"This is all a dream and now I'm proof, dreams do come true. And we are all going to make up for the time we missed out on. Our life together has just begun." I squeezed Layne's hand so he could experience the transfer of energy from my heart to his.

"They sure do, sweetheart." Layne rubbed the tips of our noses together as he spoke to me with happiness and love in eyes. He turned to the group. "Now if everybody's ready, we'll meet y'all back at the penthouse in about an hour."

After the guards scanned the area for any onlookers who might not understand an entire group of people who disappeared into thin air, the wedding party faded from sight on their way back to the reception.

Layne opened the door to the carriage and stepped back for me to enter. We settled in for our first alone time as a married couple. As the driver put the team into motion, I glanced back at the church for one last image of the place where we were wed. The magical place where we made our sacred pledges to each other.

Movement caught my eye. Had one of the guards stayed behind to make sure all was well? I gasped as I recognized the man leaning against the corner of the church. "Oh no. No, no, no."

23

Layne followed my stare to the man who had upset me so. Allvis. "Dammit! Well, that answers our big question. He *is* alive. But how? I don't understand it. That iron poker I shoved through his gut should have put an end to him forever."

"Ignore him. He would like nothing better than for us to interrupt our wedding day and you to come after him. I realize not thinking about him won't make him go away but we can't give him the satisfaction of thinking he has ruined our special day." I was determined to take control of every possible aspect of this situation. We could go chasing after him in our wedding attire and what a sight that would be.

Maybe we'd find success, or we could treat him like a spoiled child and not give in to him and provide him the satisfaction of knowing he got his way by behaving badly. Ignore the temper tantrum and take away the power.

"You're right. Nothing's changed. We never were able to say for sure he was dead and gone. Now we're sure he's not, but it doesn't matter. We'll deal with him in time. Right now, it's our time. I do need to alert Lake and Daddy so they will be aware of this latest development." He paused to allow me to speak my piece. Somehow, he knew his new wife would have a piece to speak.

I put on my best authoritative voice to share my thoughts. "I realize the guard teams must stay informed. I would prefer it if no one altered any plans for today and everyone stayed at the penthouse to celebrate with us." I paused for any forthcoming objections, but there were none.

Layne nodded for me to continue. "You have thirty seconds to relay the message before I kiss you." I smiled, raised a brow, and started to count off the time by holding up one finger at a time.

Layne chuckled and said, "Yes, ma'am," before he closed his eyes to *speak* with his daddy and Lake.

I was relieved the carriage had not exploded, there had been no thug army attacks, or kidnappings in the minutes since we had confirmed Allvis was still alive. All were tricks of his from our recent past. All were foiled by Layne and the guard teams but painful and troublesome, nonetheless.

Now, I was concerned about any new plans he might have cooked up, but I had spelled out my expectations for the day. I had to put him out of my mind and follow my own wishes if I expected everyone else to do so.

Today, we celebrate. Layne and I would leave tonight for our extended surprise honeymoon and any resolution on our Allvis situation would be left to deal with later.

"Well. I'm waiting." Layne tapped his foot on the floor with expectations of his own.

I dragged myself from my thoughts and smiled as I leaned over to fulfill my promise of a kiss. Desire seared through me as our lips touched. The passion had doubled, tripled since our kiss at the church. Our hearts were always one, but the attraction had intensified with our exchange of vows. I reached to close the curtains over the windows for privacy and turned to the loving eyes of, my husband.

We sat in silence for a moment before I slipped the shoulder of my dress down. Layne smiled and sat back to wait patiently for my next move. Thanks to Cloi and her excellent fashion design skills, the bodice of the dress fluttered to my waist. One quick snap and I was able to step from the dress in a single, graceful move.

Layne took in every inch of his new bride with adoration in his eyes before he spoke. "Mmm, you enticing woman." He swept my hair behind my shoulder and circled my neck to bring me closer. Our lips brushed together as we both inhaled the fragrance of our own heaven. The passion deepened as our lips touched, the wait was over.

"Lose the suit, cowboy," I whispered against his lips as I tugged at the buttons on his shirt only to have them disappear from my fingers. His suit now hung in a neat fashion at the back of the carriage, as did my dress.

Layne eased me down on the seat and held me as he continued his exploration of my eyes. "I love you, Mrs. Brady."

"I love *you,* too Mr. Brady and I want you. *Now.*"

He smiled. "Yes, ma'am."

We made love as the carriage gently rocked back and forth over the road. Our union was complete.

24

Our carriage drew to a stop at the penthouse I suspected since we had no other stops planned. We remained wrapped in each other's arms and I never wanted to let go. We did, however, have a group of people waiting for us upstairs.

"I don't want to get dressed." I put up a bit of a protest. I would never tire of the sizzle of excitement I experienced every time we touched.

"I do understand, but—"

"I know. We need to get upstairs and celebrate with our family and friends." I hesitated and clung tight to the warmth and strength of his body.

"I can help speed the dressing process if you like."

"Please do. But I want us to take our time getting undressed tonight. If that's possible."

"It sounds like an adventure in patience and I'm not sure I have that kind of patience, Mrs. Brady." He trailed a finger from my throat to the midpoint between my breasts.

"Hmm, we'll see who can hold out longest." I smiled, raised my chest, and took in a deep breath.

"Sounds like a contest of wills."

"A contest I'm losing right now." I wiggled beneath him and pressed closer, offering myself to him again. An advance readily accepted. He slipped his hand behind my knee, raised my leg against the seat, and settled himself as we made love again. Would I ever be satisfied? It seemed doubtful at this moment. We had waited twenty years to be together and that meant we had twenty years of loving to make up for.

Another hour passed before we were dressed and, on our way up in the elevator to make our grand entrance.

The party was in full swing, as per my wishes. Our family held their glasses high as we entered from the elevator and welcomed us as husband and wife.

Cloi met us with glasses of our own. "Come, you two. It's time for the toast from your family.

Everyone gathered and took turns toasting and wishing the happy couple the best life had to offer. No one even mentioned Allvis or the looming threat he presented. Good. This day was ours.

"Time for cake." Lake announced waving the knife in the air.

We took our places behind the cake mountain and posed for more pictures. Several photographers had been snapping away since early this morning. The wedding album promised to be enormous.

As the evening progressed to night, friends from Texas said their goodnights and headed on their way. The guards tried their best all night to keep their comings and goings secret from me, but I knew they were working a regular patrol pattern. Someone would always try and distract me as a team left or reentered the room. I'd shake a playful finger at them and get a smile in return.

"How will I ever repay everyone here who did so much to make this day so special for us?" I shook my head. Still amazed at the outpouring of love and support.

"No one expects to be repaid for a labor of love, my darlin' wife."

"Well, just let any one of them drop a hint about getting married and I'll be their wedding planner."

"And they will love it. And speaking of something to love, are you about ready to leave for the first leg of our honeymoon?"

"Sure. Where are we going?"

"Uh, uh, ah." Layne smiled and waved a finger in the air, putting a stop to my questions. "It's a surprise." He cleared his throat in an attention getting manner. "Folks, thank you all for being here and loving and supporting us today. Lynzi and I are about to leave and will be gone for a while on our extended honeymoon."

After hugs and kisses from everyone in the room, Layne secured me to his chest in a loving embrace and started our life together in whirlwind of motion. Our destination would be revealed to me shortly.

I tried not to allow thoughts of Allvis to enter my mind, but some thing's just couldn't be avoided.

He was out there.

Somewhere.

25

I opened my eyes to total darkness and glanced from side to side. "Layne, where are we?" I remained wrapped in his loving arms, a position I would be more than happy to hold for eternity if there weren't *other positions* I loved being in with him as well.

"At home." He announced.

"Home? The ranch? Brady Hill?" We now called several places home, so it was getting hard to keep up.

"You'll be able to see more tomorrow but for now—" He waved a hand in the air and dozens of candle flames flickered and illuminated the balcony area of a home I had not seen before.

"Where in the world are we?"

"North Alabama. The foothills of the Great Smoky Mountains." Layne made a sweeping gesture with his hand across the horizon.

"Foothills?" I turned to the balcony rail to get an idea of our location. Crickets chirped and lightning bugs flitted and fluttered about with intermittent flickers. Soothing night nature melodies floated on the air, but no other sounds could be heard otherwise, no traffic, no voices, just pure quiet. My kind of peace and Layne was fully aware of this. The sound of silence was perfect for our first night together as a married couple.

"You'll get the full tour tomorrow but right now; how would you feel about relaxing in a bath?" He tilted his head to his right as his hand swept through the air and additional candles flickered bright.

I turned to find an old-fashioned, claw foot bathtub filled to the rim with frothy bubbles. Red rose petals were sprinkled in a trail from our feet to the tub and rested on the mounds of fluffy suds. "A bath sounds like heaven," I exhaled as I stretched up to brush the lips of my brand-new husband.

He led the way to the tub. A second wave of his hand and we were undressed, ready for the warm bath. We stepped over the side and sank slowly into the bubbly water. Layne eased his hands around my waist and clasped his fingers together, sliding me into his embrace. I rested my head against his chest and listened to nature's evening music serenade us on our wedding night.

Cuddled in the tub as husband and wife was like nothing I had ever experienced before in my entire life. We had enjoyed each other's company in a bath in the past few weeks, but a total and *complete* feeling engulfed me at this moment. Unbelievable.

I reached for the glasses of rosebud wine on the tray beside the tub. Layne took his and as I retrieved mine, I noticed a note on the tray.

I puffed the bubbles from my fingers and unfolded the card. The air rushed from my lungs as if I'd been punched in the chest. My arm dropped onto the edge of the tub.

"Lynzi? What's wrong darlin'?"

"He's been here." I closed my eyes and wondered if Allvis would suddenly leap from the shadows and destroy us both where we sat.

Layne slid the note from my limp fingers and read it.

"Congratulations to the happy couple. Enjoy your love nest. While you can."

A guttural sound thundered from deep in Layne's chest. He crushed the card in his fist and hurled it across the balcony, bouncing it off the rail on the far side. Water splashed over the side of the tub and splatted onto the floor. "There's *no way* he was here. No way he knew about this place," Layne growled. "Aunt Pet made sure it was secure! No other human or Fae would be allowed through the veil of security."

We sat in silence for a few minutes. I sipped my wine and thought about our situation. What was our best course of action? I had absolutely no answers.

"Lynzi?"

"Hmm."

"I never intended––" He huffed out a breath and leaned his head back on the tub with a thump. His unspoken frustration rang out loud and clear.

"Stop it, Layne. You don't need to tell me you never intended to be stalked by a madman. But that happens to be a fact of our life right now. The question is, what are we going to do about it? Go after him? Where? We don't have a clue. We were determined yesterday to continue with our plans and not allow him to rob us of anymore of our life than he already has. Have you changed your mind?" I replenished the air in my lungs and continued my declaration. "I believe in Aunt Pet. This place is secure, and I intend to enjoy it."

Layne was silent. Wow. Had I just blasted him for something beyond his control? I decide to take a few minutes before I spoke again. I leaned against his chest, opened my ears, and my mind to the night sounds of the woods. The crickets, frogs, and night birds all sang their songs.

"I just can't figure him out. I even rearranged our travel plans. This location was not originally on the top of the list. No one else knew we were coming here first."

"So, he has eyes and ears all over?" And then it hit me. I sat up in the tub and turned to face my husband. Layne's expression mirrored mine. It was one of those, *why didn't I think of this before* expressions.

"The animals," we echoed at the exact same time.

We had discovered birds with a much too keen interest in our activities at the ranch several weeks ago. Aunt Pet confirmed these birds were under an enchantment spell. Our best guess was Allvis was keeping an eye on the family activity through the eyes of the birds. Could that be the case now? Was it conceivable to think he had enough power to enchant every animal in the world?

We eased back into our snuggled position. Layne finally spoke. "Ignoring him is not going to make him go away but we can't allow him to ruin our time together. I'll relay what we found to the family and hope they can come up with a plan. Tonight is our wedding night. We deal with Allvis later. For now . . ." He extended one arm, hand outstretched, fingers splayed, moving in circles. His fingers relaxed, his hand rested on the side of the tub, ". . . we are shielded from any prying eyes, human, animal, or other."

His free arm sank into the water at our side and found its way around me again. He raised one foot, turning the warm water to a slow and steady flow with his toes.

Layne was right. No solution to our Allvis problem was in sight tonight. Tonight was our night. Our wedding night.

I wondered what other surprises he had in store for me but decided to enjoy what I had in my reach at this moment . . . Layne and a bubble bath.

And here we are.

Living the dream.

Don't miss out!

Visit the website below and you can sign up to receive emails whenever Larynn Ford publishes a new book. There's no charge and no obligation.

https://books2read.com/r/B-A-XIUDB-ZYCCF

BOOKS2READ

Connecting independent readers to independent writers.

Did you love *Dreams Do Come True*? Then you should read *In My Wildest Dreams*[1] by Larynn Ford!

[2]

When she becomes the victim of several life-threatening incidents all in one week, it seems fate is out to put an end to Lynzi Lancaster. Her close calls with death trigger a series of dreams about a magical place and a certain man who broke her heart twenty years ago, Layne Brady. Could her life get any stranger? When the star of her dreams announces, in person, that he had faked his death for twenty years in order to protect her, oh, and that he's not actually human, the fireworks begin. Does she believe his extraordinary story of another world, the

---

1. https://books2read.com/u/3yX52p

2. https://books2read.com/u/3yX52p

magical world of the Fae? Do fairies really exist? Should she trust her heart? Could her dreams come true?

Read more at www.larynnford.com.

Also by Larynn Ford

The Dream Trilogy
In My Wildest Dreams
Dreams Do Come True

Standalone
Into the Light
Into the Light
Rescued
Magic in the Air

Watch for more at www.larynnford.com.

About the Author

Larynn Ford began reading romance in her early teens and became interested in writing in high school. She's a daydreamer and a romantic who is intrigued by fantasy and the paranormal. She loves to let her mind wander, always searching for a happily ever after ending to her dreams.

Besides writing, she loves gardening, spending time with her family and kitties, Evy and Ivy.

Read more at www.larynnford.com.